Has Anyone Seen My Doppelgänger?

T. Joseph Dwornicki

DORRANCE
PUBLISHING CO
EST. 1920
PITTSBURGH, PENNSYLVANIA 15238

Dorrance Publishing Co
585 Alpha Drive
Suite 103
Pittsburgh, PA 15238
Visit our website at *www. dorrancebookstore.com*

ISBN: 979-8-88683-637-0
eISBN: 979-8-88683-638-7

CHAPTER ONE

"Hey look, what's that up there in the sky?" cried James. (James, insisted strictly on being called James and not Jim or Jimmy, as that was his name) was the self-proclaimed leader of the four misfits, or outsiders if you like, that kept to themselves.

"Where?" demanded Jenny. She was the only girl in the gang. She had nerves of steel and was apparently not very afraid of much, so they all let her in.

"There!" cried James as he pointed to the northeast. The skies were filled with heavy clouds. It was late evening and darkness was rapidly filling the area around them. The clouds however, began glowing an orangish color which became brighter and brighter. Then suddenly, whoosh…

An unidentified object burst through the cloud and soared over their heads. It dropped suddenly towards the sand dunes of a lake that bordered the north section of town. They hear a soft dull thud as it landed.

"It must have landed by the lake somewhere. Let's go find it!" cried Jenny excitedly.

"You can go but I'm late for supper," complained Miles who was the fraidy-cat of the bunch.

"You're coming, like it or not Miles," growled James.

"Oh, all right. But if anything happens, I'm out of there."

"No way! This is a big deal. We should get all the credit, "said Jenny.

Gary, the last of the four, was a follower and he shook his head in agreement.

It was lucky for them that it was dinnertime, so it was possible that they were the only ones to witness the incident.

"All right, but let's hurry it up so I won't get into any more trouble at home," whined Miles. They hurried off as fast as they were able to the edge of the brackish lake forming the northern boundary of their coastal town.

But when they got there, there was no evidence of any kind that anything had happened at all. There was some disturbance in the sand on the face of the largest dune along the shore, but that could have been made by any of the wildlife found in the woods nearby. The giddiness at finding a world-changing discovery faded quickly away.

It's getting way too dark to look any further tonight," groused a disappointed Jenny.

"But I know that we all saw something fall from the sky and land here." said Gary.

"I agree, it's getting late. Tomorrow is Saturday. Let's meet at our usual time and place and go on from there." said James. The usual place was a rundown sort of convenience store that sold little in the way of groceries, but it was stocked with their favorite treats and soda. The four of them met at the store every Saturday morning to start the weekend.

They broke up then left for home. Jenny lived the closest and was the first to arrive at home. Her family already had eaten their supper and she found her mother sitting at the kitchen table going through this month's bills.

"You're late, young lady. Dinner is over. Make yourself a plate of leftovers. Then come and sit down and eat," said Jenny's mother. Jenny did as she was told, then she sat across from her mother at the table.

"Well, you're late in getting home from school tonight," observed Jenny's mother. Everything okay?" she asked.

"Okay," replied Jenny.

"Okay? That's not even a complete sentence, let alone an answer. Is everything all right at school?" asked her mother.

"Everything's fine," replied Jenny.

"Did anything unusual or interesting happen with you or any of your friends?"

"Nope."

"Finish your food, then go up to your room and finish your homework. If you finish in time, you may watch some television," said her mother. Jenny went up but she did not come back downstairs. She was not interested in watching any television.

Instead, she crawled into bed, then propped herself with some pillows so she could look out towards the lake. It was still cloudy and calm outside. Perhaps all would be revealed in the bright sunlight.

The rest of the squad was having trouble falling asleep also. James was having the most difficultly so he pulled his writing desk over to his window so that he too could look towards the lake. His brain was swirling with all sorts of *possibilities* and questions.

Would they find themselves face to face with the alien monster, and how would you capture one anyway? Would it be able to speak our language? If it asked to see our leader, who would that be anyway? James would be his spokesman.

After some time, James brought out his telescope that he had received for his birthday, then placed it on the desk. He trained it on the lakeshore, but he couldn't make out anything through the inky darkness. Searching as he did, there was no clue for him to discover. His mind was simply reeling. After all, this was not the big city with excitement around every corner. It was a small sleepy town where the weather was often the biggest news.

CHAPTER TWO

"James, are you going to lie in bed all day? Do your chores and then you can meet up with your friends. What do you want for breakfast?" yelled his mother to his bedroom.

"Just some oatmeal and some juice please," replied James.

"It'll be ready for you when you get down here," said his mother. James jumped out of his bed, threw on some old clothes, then raced downstairs for his breakfast.

"What's the big rush today? You have something pressing going on today?" asked James' mother.

"I want to make sure that I meet up with Gary and the others," explained James. He gulped down his meal and cleared his dishes. He grabbed a paper bag containing some 'things' that he might need later. He hurried out the back porch door, leaving the screen door to slam closed behind him.

James mounted his bike then pedaled furiously towards the convenience store until he arrived at the store. Gary and Miles were already there, waiting for Jenny and himself. They had placed their bikes against the light post and were sitting on the curb. That was where all of the important matters were discussed.

James put down his bike and was about to enter the store when Jenny came speeding up to the shop. James who had just arrived himself, sneered at Jenny.

"You're late!" scolded James.

"Sorrreee!" Jenny sarcastically replied. "I couldn't sleep all last night and it wasn't until morning that I could fall asleep.

"I'm going inside," said James and he went inside the store. Jenny followed him in. Soon after, all four of them were sitting on the curb, talking excitedly and at once.

"Whoa, whoa… one at a time," said James. "What was it you said, Gary?"

"I suggest that we just go back and start our search where we left off last night," said Gary.

"And let's not act as if we're not doing anything suspicious," warned James.

"That's pretty good coming from you, James," chided Jenny. "You always have this guilty look on your face."

"Hardee – har-har-har, could you be any funnier?" moaned James. But there was some truth to that statement. James had a long, thin face, tightly curled hair, and beady eyes that gave him a certain 'look.'

"It's getting late, so we need to get going now. Coming, Miles?"

"I don't know… "

They got on their bikes, then headed straight for the sand dunes they were searching around the night before. They crisscrossed the area, combing the grounds for any type of clue. But there were none to be found.

"We're wasting our time here," whined Gary. "All I could find were our tracks that we made ourselves last night."

"I know that this is where we saw that 'thing' come down," he cried. "Let's head for the school playground and mess around there for a while and have some fun," said Jenny. They grabbed their bikes and prepared to ride off. But before they had gotten very far…

"Hey, look at this! There is a set of footprints that we missed," exclaimed Jenny. There were indeed some prints in the the sand leading towards town. They were very strange looking.

They appeared to be human, but not human. The four of them followed the prints until they came to a back alleyway at the edge of town.

"Oh no! I don't believe this! The trail stops again," Jenny moaned. Because the alleyway was made of asphalt the trail disappeared. They all groaned in unison from disappointment.

"There's a space alien monster on the loose and we have no way to track it," said James.

"Well, since we're here, maybe we could check the backyards along the alley," Gary offered. They all agreed, even Miles, to search people's yards. They searched each and every property along the way. But they could not find even the hint of a clue. The mystery only grew more mysterious.

"Now what?" asked Gary.

"We might as well head for the playground like we said and plan out our next move," James said. They headed off, but they walked alongside their bikes instead of riding them so that they could talk among themselves.

When they came to the school, where the playground was located, a sizable crowd of adults had already congregated there. The grownups were very upset, and there were many loud and angry words. The children headed for the swing set while pretending not to be interested so that they could eavesdrop on the conversations.

"This means that we will have to lock our doors even during the day!" griped one grownup.

"Who could do such terrible things anyway? I never thought that I would see this day! What was taken anyway?" asked another.

"Somebody raided Mister G's garden, then the same someone snatched some clothes from his neighbor's clothesline as they were drying," grumbled yet another. The children listened in stunned silence, and they began to wonder if the space monster was behind it all.

Then something really weird happened. Farmer Jenson strolled up to a nearby tree, then leaned up against it without saying a single word. He wore a completely blank look on his face. The crowd stopped and stared at him. Farmer Jenson gave no recognition.

He usually came there at the same time every day, come rain or shine.

But today there was something really different about him. Whenever Mister Jensen came, he was usually dressed in the same way. That was, he wore a red and white plaid flannel shirt over which he wore bib overalls, calf-high, black leather boots, and a straw Panama hat on his head.

To everyone's total amazement, he stood there wearing a blue and green paisley shirt.

Along with that, he had on a pair of blue jeans that were much too short; instead of boots, he wore a pair of mismatched socks and a pair of sneakers. It fairly hurt one's eyes to look at him. It was enough to stop all of the conversation around him.

It was also about the time of day that a black Labrador dog name Ole Blue would come running up to Mister Jensen, begging for a treat that he had hidden in a pocket for him to eat. It was usually a stick of beef jerky or something similar to it.

Ole Blue came running up to the farmer like he normally did, but he skidded to a quick stop. Ole Blue began to snarl and growl menacingly at Mister Jensen who did not produce any treats at all. In fact, he did not move a single muscle. Ole Blue's owner grabbed him by his collar and took him away.

"Did you see that! Ole Blue never growled at him like before, Mister Jensen never acted so unfriendly as that before," said Jenny.

"And did you see how funny he dressed?" asked Gary.

After the excitement with Ole Blue had died down, the crowd grumbled angrily once again. No one could remember this kind of excitement before.

"Well, I don't know what the deal with the stolen clothes is about but I think that we can safely conclude that our space monster was probably hungry and took some food from people's yards," said Jenny.

"But what if the space whatever it is, only eats humans and what he took was just the appetizer?" asked Miles.

"You know what, Miles?" said James.

"What?"

"I understand now why your parents name you Miles, putting the s at the end of your name instead of the front. You are always so negative," said James.

"Well, how do you know that he, if it is a he, isn't planning to put the whole town under his mind control? Look at Farmer Jensen. He was acting really, really weird. How do I know whether or not he hasn't gotten control of your minds?" Miles asked the group.

"Because you still look like a doofus," laughed Jenny.

"I really need to get back home. Let's come up with a real plan of action over the weekend. "Let's meet on the school playground before we go inside," James suggested. Then they all went home.

CHAPTER THREE

Monday couldn't come soon enough for the four friends. They found them-selves on the swing set, comparing notes.

"Anything new since last Friday?" asked James.

"Nothing on my end," said Jenny.

"My parents think an outsider came into town riding a railroad car. He snuck into town and stole some food because he was hungry. Then he took some clothes because his own were worn out. Afterwards he got back to the rails and left," said Gary.

"I don't believe that for a second," said Jenny. They talked some more but the school bell interrupted their discussion.

"We should talk at the shop after school where we can talk in private," said James, rather quietly.

The fourth graders took their usual assigned desk and waited for their teacher, Miss Peachtree.

Miss Peachtree strode into the classroom, then quietly shut the door behind her.

"I trust that you finished your essays over the weekend despite all the disturbances going around," said Miss Peachtree. There was a great deal of grumbling from her students.

"There has been a number of incidents that has happened over the last couple of days," she said,

Our principal has asked that we warn you to keep yourselves safe and to watch out for any strangers here at school. In the meantime, please pass your papers to the front desk in your row," said Miss Peachtree.

The day dragged on and on for the four classmates. They were totally unable to concentrate on their studies. Throughout the morning and throughout the afternoon, they constantly gave each other knowing glances. But the day did end and the four of them headed straight for the convenience store to get some snacks and to talk.

"My parents are all up in arms about the thefts that happened over the weekend. I don't think that it was just some stranger that snuck into town, stole some stuff, then hid out again," said Jenny.

"Let's get organized," said James. "I think the first thing we need to do is make a list of the things we do know," he added. They looked at each other as nobody wanted to be the secretary.

"Miles, you have a notebook with you, right?" asked James.

"Mmmph!" grumbled Miles. He opened his backpack until he found a notebook and a pencil. He turned to the middle of the book and waited for the things to be written down.

"First, we saw a flying space thingy. It landed somewhere near the dunes of the lake," said Jenny.

"Next, we found a pair of strange footprints that led to the alley," said James.

"Which we lost," said Miles.

"People began complaining about missing clothes and food. They blame it on some mysterious stranger that nobody ever saw," said Gary.

"And what about Mister Jensen? He didn't act his normal self last Saturday. And look how Ole Blue barked at him as if he didn't recognize him and had to be dragged away by Bobby," said Jenny.

"Maybe he was being controlled by the space monster or maybe… it wasn't Mister Jensen at all who was eaten by the space alien!" bawled Miles.

"Now what? We can't tell our parents because they will either laugh in our faces or they will put us in our rooms and keep us there until we're teenagers!" whined Jenny.

"How about I ask Bobby if we might borrow Ole Blue for an hour or two? I'll bet he could recognize the alien," said Gary.

"What good is that if we don't know where to look?" asked James.

"Well, I was thinking that Ole Blue could follow the alien's trail by following his scent," proposed Gary.

"Do you think Bobby will let us? What are you going to use a reason for borrowing Ole Blue?" asked Jenny.

"I'll think of something. Just meet me at the lake tomorrow afternoon and we'll see how good of a bird dog Ole Blue is," Gary said.

"We'd better do it soon. The trail is already growing cold. Tomorrow first thing, we should get home before our parents freak out and start yelling at us," James said.

Chapter Four

James and the rest met at the lakeshore where the alien footsteps began. Gary had Bobby's dog Blue, in hand. Once everyone was present, Gary brought the dog over to the prints and had him sniff them. Blue started to yelp and yip quite rabidly at them.

"It looks like the trail is still warm," James remarked. Gary let out some slack on Blue's leash, then urged him on to follow the space monster's tracks.

At first Ole Blue backed away from the alien's scent but because of the children's insistence, he was convinced to follow the still viable scent. Gary forced the reluctant dog's nose to the ground and they started off.

"Look he's going forward. We're off to capture a space alien!" cried an excited Jenny.

Ole Blue swept his head back and forth until they came to the paved section of the alley. Ole Blue hesitated for a brief moment, then he went forward once again. Suddenly, he ducked into the first yard to their left.

"He went in there," cried James excitedly as Ole Blue zigged and zagged crazily back and forth across the yard until he suddenly left the yard, then he ran into the yard directly across the way. The dog repeated the same confusing pattern as before.

Ole Blue led them into the next yard, then the next, and the next. There was one yard left on the block, and the dog led them there also.

"Look, the alien went in here too!" cried James.

"What yard didn't he go into?" complained Miles.

"Hey, you kids get out of my yard before I call the sheriff!" threatened an angry homeowner.

"We're going, mister. Sheesh, we'll never track the space monster at this rate," groused Jenny.

"Gary, why don't you go on ahead and return Blue to Bobby and thank him for us?" Obviously, we can't go into everybody's yard in town. We need to come up with a better plan. I'm tired and I want to go home now. I'll see you all at school tomorrow," James said sadly.

Later that night, as Jenny lay in her bed, she gazed out of her bedroom window and up into the starry night sky. She wondered if there was really a space monster or if they had really witnessed anything at all.

But, if there were really a spaceship, what would its pilot look like? From what galaxy did he come from if it were a he? Why was he here in the first place? What would he want?

The real question was where would he be hiding? Then Jenny realized that she had forgotten to do her homework. She would have to try and finish it in the morning before school started. When James arrived at home, his father began to question him about his whereabouts that afternoon.

"There has been a lot of thefts that has taken place around town lately. Would you or any of your friends have anything to do with it? Or maybe one of you might have any information we would like to know?" asked James' father.

"No, we don't Dad," replied James. That statement was at least partially true because neither they nor anyone else for that matter actually saw what happened.

"We need your promise not to get involved, James, or there will be heck to pay," demanded his mother.

"I promise, I promise!" replied James.

Things didn't settle down at all. In fact, they heated up to the point that Deputy Smith was forced to add an additional might patrol after dark. The timing was quite unfortunate as the sheriff was away on official business at the state capital, and there was no way of telling when he would be returning.

Things really came to a head when on Friday afternoon, before class dismissal Miss Peachtree gave out some flyers to all of the front desks in the classroom.

"Pass the sheets to the desks behind you now. Please give these to your parents at home. These papers explain the new temporary rules the principal has issued to keep the students safe from harm. You don't need to have your parents sign them, but make sure that they receive them. Have a good evening," said the teacher.

The four friends met in the schoolyard before going home.

"Ugh! Look at this! The playground is off limits to us kids until further notice. They want our parents to drop us off at school if at all possible. If we walk to school, we can't be by ourselves. We have to have a 'buddy' with us at all times. There is a bunch of other stuff in here. I guess we won't be seeing much of each other until this thing ends. We'd better find the space monster soon or we won't be able to do anything," moaned Jenny.

"Let's keep in touch by way of the telephone, but don't say anything about a space monster or anything else because they will all be listening in on our conversations," said Jenny.

"Yeah, my little sister would love to get me in any kind of trouble," griped Gary. They tried to call each other but it was not very satisfying. They could only have one way conversations, and that was not very satisfying because they were used to being in each other's company.

Worse yet, none of them could talk about the one and only subject that they were interested in.

Came Monday and they could not communicate with each other before classes. At least they could talk at lunch time and since they considered themselves as outsiders, they usually sat at a table in the back of the lunchroom. There at least they could be by themselves.

"What do we do now, the law will probably not catch the thief if it is our alien visitor?" asked James.

"Yeah, we kids can't ever be alone now with the grownups watching our every movement," complained Gary.

"Well, I personally feel safer," said Miles. They were pretty much silent throughout the rest of the lunch period. But their frustration didn't end there.

At the end of the school day, Miss Peachtree, their teacher, had another announcement for them.

"I have some notices for you to give your parents to read. Give them to your parents right away. Have a good night and we'll begin again tomorrow," she said.

CHAPTER FIVE

What the students brought home was a notice of a townhall meeting at the local Veterans Hall concerning the local crime wave. This was a small town where everybody knew each other and it was quite unsettling that there was someone in their midst who was capable of such terrible deeds.

When Jenny gave her notice to her father, he read it aloud for the whole family to hear. It would occur on a night and time that he could attend.

"If it's that important, maybe I should go. I have never attended an emergency townhall meeting before, and probably neither has anyone else in this town. This might be the event of a lifetime," said Jenny's father.

Now Jenny was not about to let an opportunity to spend a rare evening with her dad go by. Jenny begged her dad to let her go with him.

"I want to come too," she said.

"I don't know, Jenny," said her mother. "It's on a school night and there is no way of knowing beforehand how long the meeting will go."

"Please? I will have my homework done and my chores too. Pretty please, I don't get don't get to spend much time with Dad, and besides, I might learn something I might be able to use later in life. Pretty please?"

"Well, when you put it that way, I guess it would be all right. Let's have dinner before it gets cold," said her mother.

The meeting was held the very next night. Jenny rushed home to do her chores. Then she rushed upstairs to her bedroom to work on her homework. She had her dinner, after which she watched a little television while waiting for the time to go.

"Did you finish everything you were supposed to?" asked her dad.

"I did," Jenny replied.

"Then let's go." They decided to walk because her father was worried about finding a parking place. They walked there with her dad holding her hand, which made Jenny feel very happy. When they arrived, they found that almost all of the seats were taken. They were lucky enough to find two seats together located in the back of the hall. It was quite loud, and Jenny could feel the excitement.

After a time, the town's mayor Mister Todd, strode up to the front of the audience where the podium was located. He held a wooden gavel in his right hand. He stood there patiently waiting for the clock on the wall to strike eight o'clock.

Then… Bang! Bang! Bang! The gavel slammed the podium three times.

"This here meeting is about to commence! We have some serious business to discuss tonight," declared the mayor. Jenny and her father looked at each other in a serious manner.

"We are gathered here tonight in order to talk about the recent crime wave the likes of which the city has never known before. The sheriff is still away on official business at the capital and sends his regrets. So instead, I will turn the meeting over to Deputy Smith. So please give him your full attention," urged the mayor.

The meeting was about the people's concerns about the thefts and it went fairly well at first. But then they began shouting out how they saw the stranger sneaking about.

"I saw him! He was very tall and had snow white hair," yelled one lady.

"No, he was short and very stout," cried another.

"You're wrong! He was muscular and had dark hair," said one man.

Deputy Smith brought the meeting back to order.

"All right, all right! We have added night patrols. We will give you a special number to call if you see a prowler. But most importantly, we will rely on each of you to be our eyes. Don't leave anything of value outside where it can be taken. Look out for each other and we will get through this. As I call this meeting adjourned, let me remind you to take a flyer home with you. It contains that number that I mentioned and some helpful suggestions that you might want to go through," added Deputy Smith.

"Hold up a minute," said the mayor. "Before we go and while I have all of you here, it was brought to my attention the matter of our annual Halloween parade." Finally, here was something Jenny was interested in.

"Simple majority becomes the rule. Give me a show of hands," said the mayor. Someone counted the number of hands that went up. It was very, very close. "By the slim margin of only two, the motion carried. We shall have a parade again this year. Go home and be safe," added the mayor.

Jenny and her father didn't talk much on the way home. Not a lot was accomplished at the meeting. At least the Halloween parade wasn't canceled.

Jenny really wanted to tell her father about what she knew. There would be no telling how her dad would react so she kept her secret to herself.

In the morning, it was not much better. When she sat down for breakfast, she saw the newspaper sitting in the middle of the table. On the front page was a huge banner proclaiming that a terrible crimewave was overtaking the city. Jenny quickly wolfed down her oatmeal and juice, and headed off for school.

The gang wasn't able to talk among themselves until lunchtime.

"The grownups don't seem to know how to react or what to do," James complained.

"Neither do we," said Miles.

"I've been thinking about it and I suggest that we make a list of the theft reports in the order that they occurred. Then maybe discover where the monster is hiding out or maybe predict his next move," James said.

"How do we make such a list as that?" asked Miles.

"We just go to the local newspaper and have them give us a list," said James.

"I doubt that they would give us the time of day because we're only kids," griped Jenny.

"Well, where do they get their information from?" asked Gary.

"They must get it from the police station. The newspaper reporters probably call the sheriff and he gives them what to print," said James.

"Great, what makes you think that the police would talk to us either? What do we tell them when they ask why we need the information? We aren't even supposed to be on the streets by ourselves," whined Miles.

"Fine, I'll go by myself. If we let every obstacle stop us, we might just as well give up now," said Jenny.

"We can't let you do that. We'll go with you, right guys?" asked James. Nobody answered but that didn't matter.

CHAPTER SIX

If a stranger came into town looking for the police station, he or she would most likely walk right past it. The station itself was situated in the middle of the block on Main Street. It was surrounded by shops and stores, making it even harder to locate. The entrance to the station was a plain, dark brown door. Above that was a small sign on which the word POLICE was embossed.

Next to the door was a large pane window that you could not see into because the window blinds were always drawn closed.

It was on this day that the gang gathered enough nerve to visit the police station. They hopped on their bikes and pedaled to the north end of Main Street.

"Miles, you stay behind and watch our bikes while we talk to the police," James said. Miles was only too happy to oblige. They dismounted their bikes and started walking down the block.

"Try not acting like something is going on or they will get suspicious," warned James. They walked on slowly and unsure of themselves. Gary spotted the official police cruiser sitting in the front of the entrance.

"It looks as if somebody's home at least," he said. They came to the imposing door and stopped then they looked at each other.

"What now?" asked Gary.

"We go in," chided James.

"No, I mean that there is no door knocker or doorbell or anything," Gary said.

"Just try the door. If it opens, we just go inside," said Jenny.

"It's dark in there and I didn't see anybody through the window," Gary said.

"Never mind!" Jenny said. She grabbed the door handle and cautiously walked inside. It was indeed dark inside. No one was sitting in the receptionist's chair and the only light came from a back hallway.

"This place gives me the creeps," said Gary. James located a bell that you ding with your hand, just like the one found on Miss Peachtree's desk at school. He hit it a couple of times, then waited for some kind of response.

"I'll be with you in just a sec," said a voice from one of the backrooms. Before long, Deputy Smith rounded the corner, carrying a firearm in a holster in such a way so that everybody could see it.

"Say, where are your parents? What do you want anyway?" said the deputy rather impatiently.

"They are probably at home," said James after he gathered enough bravery to answer him. Jenny spoke up next.

"I see that the map of the city by the counter has a bunch of red pins sticking in it. Those must be the houses that were hit by the stranger. We would like a list of those places," Jenny said.

"That is privileged information that is reserved for the newspaper and other interested parties. You kids need to leave here and go home before I call your parents to come and get you. Now scoot," warned the deputy.

"Yes, sir," they said together. When the three of them filed out onto the sidewalk Jenny noticed that James was sort of acting strangely.

"What's that that you have under your arm, James?" Jenny asked.

"Walk first and don't look back. Just keep walking," said James.

As they caught up to Miles, James barked out an order.

"Quick head for Gary's house. I have something to show everybody!" yelped James.

"Like what?" asked Miles.

"I don't know, some sort of secret," replied Jenny. They pedaled as fast as they could before anyone would stop them. After a while, James reached into his jacket then pulled out a piece of paper that was folded in half.

"I took a list of incidents from the front counter at the police station," boasted James.

"You stole from the cops?!" cried Gary.

"Relax, there was a whole stack of them lying on the counter. Nobody will miss it."

"You'd better hope not. I will swear that I didn't see a thing," Jenny warned.

James unfolded the sheet of paper and began to trace the dots on it. It was all too confusing for them to make any real conclusion. He studied it a little while longer. Finally, something did make some sort of sense to him.

"All of these dots are just mumble-jumble. But if you look at the latest events, most of them occur around Jenny's house. Here, take a look at this. Maybe it is a place to start searching. Why don't we think of a plan at home tonight so we can discuss them at lunch tomorrow?" James said.

"Jenny said that the town was planning on holding the annual Halloween parade despite all of the uproar. How about we talk about that for a while instead of always going on about some stranger terrorizing the neighbors?" said Miles.

"I totally agree," said Jenny. "So, what are you planning to go as this year, Miles?" Miles thought for a few seconds.

"I think… I think I will go as a dinosaur. Maybe a T. Rex," he replied.

"Gary, how about you?" James asked.

"I think that it would be cool to go as a mad scientist this time," said Gary.

"And how about you, James?" asked Jenny.

"A pirate," he said. Everybody groaned.

"You go as a pirate every year," they all moaned.

"I wanna be a pirate and I'm going to go as a pirate!" said James, asserting himself.

James looked at Jenny.

"What are you going to be this year?" he asked. And without any hesitation, she said, "A space monster!"

"That should be interesting," Gary said. James said that he should go home before his parents would miss him. Thy could discuss the situation tomorrow at school.

It was a very rainy day the next day, so the four students stayed in the cafeteria to talk.

"Any new ideas on how to handle the situation?" asked James.

"Not me," grumbled Miles.

"Me neither," said Gary.

"Since the stranger seems to favor my neighborhood, I propose setting a trap in my backyard," said Jenny.

"A trap, how do you propose to do that?" asked James.

"I'm not totally sure yet, but I will set it up after Halloween," she said.

CHAPTER SEVEN

It was a tremendous stroke of luck that Halloween fell on a Saturday. Even the weather cooperated, which was not always the case, and it provided the perfect setting for trick-or-treating and a parade. The parade itself was set to begin at eight o'clock, allowing ample time for the children to visit most of the houses in their neighborhood. There were adults everywhere, keeping troublemaking down to a minimum. The whole town seemed to be out and enjoying itself. It was a very good night.

Then as advertised, the siren on an antique firetruck called everyone to the parade route.

Jenny's parents were kind enough to arrive early in order to save some spots for the children as they trick-or-treated. The first one to come was Gary, who looked every inch the mad scientist, wearing a long white lab coat and tinted goggles.

"My don't we look scary in that outfit," said Jenny's mother.

"Thanks Jenny's mom, have you seen the others?" he asked.

"They're probably trying to hit as many houses before they get here. I'm sure that they will show up soon," said Jenny's father. As soon as he had finished saying that, Miles came around the corner wearing his T. Rex costume. He had a very long tail that dragged along the ground and a very large head filled with fearsome teeth.

"Don't you look scary tonight," said Jenny's mother.

"Npphhh!" came a muffled reply from somewhere inside the reptilian head.

James and Jenny went out together, but at the last minute she had James go on ahead of her and he arrived next wearing his pirate costume. Part of the costume was a hook that took the place of his left hand.

"How did you lose your hand, captain?" joked Jenny's mother.

"He lost a fight with an angry goldfish," laughed Gary.

"That wasn't very nice, Gary."

Jenny rounded the corner just as the high school band started marching. She was wearing her space monster disguise. Her monster had an armored tail, webbed feet, and a rubbery face with big shiny teeth. The main body portion of the body had six arms that flailed in every direction, and on top all that, she was covered all over with silvery fish scales. It was quite the Halloween costume.

The firetruck sounded its siren once again and the parade started down the street. The firetruck was in the lead, and behind it were all manner of scary monsters, and alongside of them were eerily clad wizards and witches carrying black cauldrons filled with candy. They tossed the treats into the waiting arms of the crowd as they pranced by.

The high school band was in formation, waiting for their cue to begin marching on the opposite side of the street. There was a table on which there were all sorts of hot drinks and other goodies for the participants of the parade. Jenny was able to see through the band members to see what was happening there.

Out of nowhere, a stranger appeared at the table and started to shovel food into his mouth. Jenny did not recognize him, so she assumed that it was one of the parade organizers.

"Wow! Look at him chow down," said Jenny as she pointed to the table.

"Yeah! He must be starved. I don't recognize him. Anybody ever seen him before?" asked Gary. Suddenly, Jenny became very excited.

"He's the one!" exclaimed Jenny. She darted into the marching band members, weaving her way to the other side of Main Street. The stranger saw her coming and he began to run. Jenny chased him down Main Street wither her arms flapping wildly as she ran.

"What just happened?" asked Jenny's mother.

James and Gary took off after her trying to fight their way to the other side. Miles could barely move so he stayed behind. Jenny's parents rushed into the police station to get Deputy Smith.

After a moment, they all came running outside.

"Which way did they go?" asked the deputy. Miles pointed in the direction that they went. The deputy ran off in hot pursuit.

"Somebody stop him!" screamed Jenny at the very top of her voice, but she was drowned out by the music being played by the band. The only person to hear her was the stranger and he had no intention of stopping.

"Stop, you kids, what do you think you're doing?" shouted the deputy. He had only managed to catch up to Gary and James.

"Our friend Jenny there, started to run after that man there, yelling 'That's him!' and that was it," explained James.

"You kids stay back and let me handle this," cried the deputy. Then, to everyone's horror, both Jenny and the culprit turned the corner at the end of the block and disappeared.

"Oh no, she'll get hurt or worse!" yelled Gary. They rushed as hard as they could to catch up to Jenny. Then the deputy rounded the corner. He saw Jenny stopped at the entrance to a dead-end alley way. She stood there with all of her arms pointing to someone inside.

"I've got him cornered. He's inside and there is no possible way out," Jenny boasted.

Deputy Smith slowed and stopped beside Jenny. He rudely pushed her out of the way and then he drew his firearm. He warned Gary and James to go no further.

"You kids shouldn't have done this. You could have been seriously harmed. Stay back and let me handle this. Whoever you are, come on out peacefully. There is no way to escape and I am armed," warned the deputy.

There came a very loud bang and a clang as the lid of a metal trashcan rolled towards the deputy. Suddenly a black cat came racing out towards the street. The lawman produced a long flashlight from his side and he flashed it all about the walls of the alley. He detected a movement in one of the corners, then he directed the beam of light there.

"There you are! Give yourself up." A man stepped forward.

"Mister Chang!" yelled the children. Mister Chang owned the restaurant in the block nearby and it had an exit doorway that opened up in the alley. He just stood there, silent and motionless.

"Are you okay? Did you see anybody else in here?" asked the deputy. Mister Chang didn't say a word, but only shook his head no.

"I'm really sorry to have bothered you. Everybody is all worked up about this stranger. Go on about your business and we will leave you be."

He looked at the children and he scolded them.

"We are very lucky that nobody had gotten hurt. I'm telling you kids for the last time, stay out of other people's hair and go back to your parents. I'm not very happy right now. Now git!" said an unhappy Deputy Smith.

"I didn't imagine it. I saw him chowing down as if he hadn't eaten for a thousand years. I didn't lose sight of him for even a single moment. I'm telling you; I chased somebody else into that alley. There is no possible way that he could have slipped out of the alley without one of us noticing it. I'm telling you; I chased some stranger into that dead end," moaned Jenny.

"How do you explain Mister Chang's being in the alley and not the stranger that you claim it was?" asked Gary.

"I can't," protested Jenny.

"Let's forget about it and go back to what's left of the parade before we get into any more trouble tonight," said James rather sadly.

"Hey, wait a minute," said Jenny. She became somewhat excited with a sudden inspiration. "Gary or James, did either of you get a good look at what the stranger was wearing?" she asked.

"You were too far ahead of me to see," said James.

"How about you, Gary?" asked Jenny.

"I don't think so," he said.

"Think real hard. What was the storeowner wearing when he showed himself? Try to remember," said Jenny.

"Hey… that's right," Gary thought out loud.

"I'm totally confused," complained Miles.

"Maybe I can explain, but it may not help you very much, Miles. I chased a total stranger into a dead-end alley with no way out. This person was wearing a certain set of clothes. When we got there, there was no stranger. Instead, we found Mister Chang. But the odd thing was that he was wearing the stranger's clothes," explained Jenny.

"I still don't get it," said Miles.

"Well, where do we go from here?" said James.

"We set a trap," said Jenny.

"How? The adults will be watching us like hawks," said James.

"We talk at lunch Monday," Jenny said.

CHAPTER EIGHT

The next Monday, the four of them sat at their usual table and talked amongst themselves while having their meal. The idea of setting up a trap didn't seem like such a fantastic idea after the excitement on Halloween. Everybody was watching everybody else.

"Tell us your big plan, Jenny. It had better be good or else because this monster has gotten me into more trouble than I can handle," Gary griped.

"I will concede if this doesn't work out; if he is still out there, he still needs to eat and the weather is getting colder, so he may need some warmer things to wear," Jenny said.

"Yeah, so?" said James sarcastically.

"So… We set a trap using food and clothes as bait," replied Jenny.

"Where do you plan to do that? My parents would punish me from here to eternity," whined Miles.

"Don't worry about it. I will lure him to my house," she replied. The others looked at each other in complete and utter surprise.

"Your place? Why there?" asked James.

"We have an old toolshed way in the corner of our backyard. It needs some cleaning but I think it will work. Once it is cleaned and ready, we set the trap and wait for the alien to appear. But there is one little thing that I haven't worked out yet," said Jenny.

"Oh, here it comes," grumbled James.

"Hear me out. I have a problem for you to solve, James," she said. James began to swell with pride. After all, James considered himself the brains of the group.

"The success of the whole thing depends on the alien taking the bait then locking himself inside. So, what I need for you to do, James, is to figure out a lock that will prevent the alien from escaping once he's inside the toolshed," said Jenny.

"It'll be ready by Wednesday," promised James.

"All right then, my house on Wednesday. We have a space alien to capture!" Jenny boasted.

Jenny's mother picked her up after school with the family car and together they did some chores and had a chance to talk. Most of the conversation was about the trouble in town so Jenny tried to make the mood a little lighter.

"I do hope we finish soon. I have already done my homework. I would like to do some yard work and maybe clean up the shed in back," said Jenny. Her mother looked very pleased at first, then she had a very puzzled look on her face. She usually had to fight with Jenny to get her to do anything, let alone a huge chore like cleaning out the shed.

"Are you hiding something out there? That doesn't sound like something that you would volunteer for," her mother said.

"Oh, Mom. What harm can it do?" Jenny said. They finished their tasks for the day then they found their way home. But her mother was still more than a little suspicious. It was getting late in the day, so Jenny decided that it would be better to get started right away.

She opened the door to the storage shed and it immediately reeked of dirt, mulch, and used motor oil. She started to regret her plans, but was determined to show the gang that she was able to capture a space alien.

Jenny removed the trash, then she swept the floor clean. She put the tools where they belonged then stacked the rest of the things neatly in the corners. She had finished just in time as it was getting too dark to go any further. She started to become excited all over again.

She couldn't hardly wait for Wednesday evening when everything would be set. It was still a very long shot but if that didn't work nothing else would.

Jenny really hadn't given James a whole lot of time to work out a solution to the lock problem, but she had faith in James. Jenny spent her night figuring and refiguring what they must do to capture the infamous space monster.

When Wednesday came it was a whirlwind for Jenny. There was a sort of self-imposed curfew because the thefts were continuing and no one knew how to stop them. Her mother picked Jenny up with the car at school, as was recommended, then drove her home.

Jenny raced through her homework as fast as she was able. She asked her mother about when dinner would be ready. Luckily, it couldn't be anytime soon leaving Jenny time to set the trap the way she wanted. She went to the shed and waited for the others to arrive. It seemed like forever, but soon they were all together.

"We used the excuse that we were working on a project together, which is kind of the truth. We have only an hour to work before we need to head back home," said Gary.

"Okay, James, please show us what you have come up with," said Jenny.

"I need to borrow a hammer," James said. Then Jenny handed him one, then went outside with the other three following him. James pounded away and then he stepped back to let them see his handiwork.

"This is the only door in or out. The space monster smells something good to eat, then he sneaks inside to have dinner. He opens the door, not realizing that he has walked into a trap. Once he goes inside, this tripwire releases this wooden slat. The slat falls and is caught by this latch trapping the monster inside the shed," said James.

"Very impressive, but what do we use as bait?" wondered Gary.

Jenny said, "In the middle of the floor is an old TV tray. On it will be a peanut butter and jelly sandwich, along with an apple. He'll probably be thirsty, so there will be a jar filled with water. It isn't much but it was all I could sneak out without being noticed. Let's get out of here and hope that he takes our bait. It should go as planned, as long as my snoopy little brother Robert keeps to his bratty little self." Jenny shooed the gang home, then set the trap. Then she went inside where her dinner was being laid out on the dinner table.

At the dinner table, Jenny's mother remarked that she was spending quite a bit of time around the shed lately.

"I'm setting a trap for the stranger," joked Jenny, half seriously.

"That's not very funny right now. Many people are taking it seriously," warned her mother.

"I think we should go out there and see what is going on out there," laughed Robert, her smaller brother.

"Go right ahead, twerp. And if you would happen to disappear, don't look for us to go looking for you. As if anyone would miss you anyway," chided Jenny.

"Stop it, the both of you or you can spend the rest of the night in your room," warned her mother.

CHAPTER NINE

A late season thunderstorm arose that night. It caused Jenny to lay awake in her bed as she worried that the pounding rain would keep the alien monster from springing her carefully prepared trap. Fortunately for her, the claps of rolling thunder lulled her to sleep by quieting her mind. She remained that way until the break of dawn.

The sun woke Jenny before the others in her family. Unfortunately, she couldn't see the shed from her room. Jenny put on some clothes and snuck out of the back door downstairs. She had no idea of what she might find out. She gathered all of her nerves and she advanced on the shed, even though she was all by herself. Halfway to the shed, she found a wooden baseball bat lying on the ground. For once, Jenny was sort of glad that Robert was a slob. Jenny soon found herself in front of the door. The trap had been sprung! Once again, she gathered all of her resolve.

"All right, whoever or whatever you are, you must surrender! There's a bunch of us out here and we have weapons! I'm opening the door now, prepare yourself." She removed the slat that held the door shut. She raised the baseball bat over her head as she swung the door wide open. But nothing happened. There was not even the slightest sound of movement.

"I'm not asking you again! Come out and we will go easy on you." Still nothing happened. Jenny advanced to the doorway in order to poke her head inside. She was kicking herself for not bringing a flashlight along with her. Jenny waited a bit so that her eyes would have a chance to adjust to the dim light.

But then, a shaft of pale-yellow sunlight fell on the food tray revealing the fact that whoever or whatever had been inside had their fill and was not long gone.

Jenny felt relief and disappointment at the very same time. Then her mind snapped back to reality. She decided to go back inside before any of her family could see her and question her. She couldn't wait to tell the gang at school.

Jenny chose to wait until the lunchbreak to tell her story. In private.

"That was not very smart, going in there alone. How would you know whether or not the monster eats children?" asked Miles. The rest of them just groaned.

"I want to try again. Tonight!" said Jenny.

"Are you crazy? You were lucky that you didn't get hurt or in trouble," Miles warned.

"If I have to capture him by myself, I will do it, you bunch of sniveling cowards," Jenny taunted. But none volunteered.

"He escaped being captured once. What makes you think that he would risk being caught again?" asked James.

"Everybody in town has harvested their gardens. Food would be very hard to find," explained Jenny.

"If he came inside, ate the food then left, how did he escape our trap?" asked Gary. "It seems that monster still needs to eat. Just come over to my house tonight after dark so he can work on our 'project'," said Jenny. And that was what they did.

"Look for clues, everybody, he didn't just walk through the walls. That door was sealed shut," said Jenny. The four of them searched and searched but they couldn't find a single clue as to how the monster escaped the trap.

As they were about to give up, Gary felt a slight breeze coming from the wall where the work bench was located. There was a window located just above it. Jenny walked over and discovered that the window was opened just a bit.

"I feel so stupid! I thought about everything else, but I didn't think about the dumb window," moaned Jenny.

"Now what?" asked Miles.

"We set the trap up again but we make sure that he doesn't open up the window. I'm going inside to get some more food and water for the trap. Don't do anything until I return," warned Jenny. She went inside her house, then returned with a backpack in which she saved some uneaten lunch items from school.

Jenny placed the food on the tray along with some fresh water, as before.

"You have to promise me that you will come back here early in the morning so that I don't have to take any more risks by myself," she said. Then they all let out a loud groan.

"I don't want to get into any more trouble with my parents," griped Gary.

"Look it's my house, my food, and if he gets caught by my parents, I'm in a lot bigger trouble than any of you," said Jenny. The gang just looked at each other for a while.

"Oh, all right, we'll help you," they said.

They were as good as their word. It was early the next morning when Jenny heard some pebbles hit her bedroom window. Jenny looked at her alarm clock. It was 4:30 in the morning. She slowly opened her window and saw James standing directly beneath it. She stuck her head out and began to whisper quietly to the others below.

"What's wrong? What happened?"

"Gary heard some dogs barking and they seemed to end up at your place. We snuck out and now we are here to see if there's somebody in your yard," whispered James.

"I'll be right down after I grab a light and Robert's baseball bat," replied Jenny. She grabbed what she wanted, then crept down the stairs and out into the backyard. She led them to the shed, then she shined the light on the door. To their amazement and excitement, they found that the trap had been sprung.

"Everybody, grab something to defend yourself with in case he comes after you," cautioned Jenny. They surrounded the opening to the shed, and they gazed at each other with frightened looks.

"Ready, guys?" Hold up your bats while I crack open the door. Ready… here it goes." This time, Jenny thew the door open quickly. They could neither see nor hear anything. She shone her light on the food tray. The food was gone as before. Then she shone her light in each of the corners but could not see anything. She checked the window. It was still sealed shut.

"You can come on in, he's escaped again," moaned Jenny.

"Are you sure that you did everything right? The monster sure knows how to make fools of us. I think we should quit," said Miles.

"Me too," said Gary. But Jenny went around and around looking for something. Then suddenly her foot went right through the floor. He or it or whatever it was had escaped by going beneath the shed.

"I want to try one more time. It will be the absolute last time, I swear!" begged Jenny.

"I just wanted to go home before someone discovered that I'm missing," whined Gary.

"Please… please… please… please. . .," begged Jenny. "We know he is real, and we can't get back to normal until he is caught," said Jenny.

"One last time and that's it! I don't need any more drama," said Gary.

"My family usually gets up by seven or eight in the morning. Come by no later than five. When I get home later today, I will fill in the area underneath the shed and set the bolt one last time," said Jenny.

"We had better get out of here. I really don't need any more excitement or trouble from anyone else," said Gary.

Later that evening, the trap was set once again.

CHAPTER TEN

Jenny had difficulty sleeping. One time she gazed at her alarm clock and it read 4:00. She figured that it wouldn't pay to try and sleep then, so she put on a heavy jacket then silently made her way to the back steps to wait the arrival of the others. It was overcast and cold, and it looked as if snow was on the way.

Jenny had been quite clever in that she had put warm clothes in the shed as part of the trap, because she thought that whoever the culprit was needed heavier clothing to wear, even if he was no longer looking for food.

The other three showed up shortly. This time, they were well armed with bats.

"This is the very last time, Jenny," James warned. They headed for the shed. As they neared the shed, they saw that the trap had been sprung yet again. Jenny went around to the side window, then shone her light inside. The food used as bait was gone, as well as the clothing.

"He's been here," whispered Jenny. Then she joined the others at the front door of the shed. James carefully lifted the slat that held the door closed form its berth. He slowly opened the door, not really expecting anything.

"Give me that light," said James and he flashed all about.

"Just as I thought, nothing," James said. Suddenly a rake that had been stacked in the corner fell with a frightening bang.

"Somebody's in there!" exclaimed Miles. "I'm not going in there!"

"I told you it would work," said Jenny. James directed the light in the direction from which the racket came from. There was a pause, then slowly a figure emerged from the dark.

The so-called monster looked exactly like Jenny! They all gasped at the same time. They all stood looking at each other.

"You're the monster, Jenny?" cried Miles.

"Get real! This is what my father would call a doppelgänger," said Jenny.

"A what?" asked Gary.

"It's some kind of spook that can look like other people," James said.

Jenny walked up to the stranger so that she would be face to face with him or her. They were mirror images of each other, even down to Jenny's freckles.

"You had better tell us what you are doing here, or it will go badly for you," warned Jenny. "Where are you from?" she asked. The other Jenny pointed out the window and up towards the Big Dipper.

"So, you are from outer space," said James. But before they could ask any more questions, Gary saw a light go on in Jenny's kitchen and sounded the alarm.

"Get out of here before anyone sees us. We should all meet here later this afternoon so as not to attract any more attention than necessary. My other self, you need to stay out of sight. We'll try to hide and protect you, but you need to stay hidden. I'll bet that you are still hungry. I'll try to sneak out some food to you later," said Jenny. Then she went inside.

Her mother was making breakfast for the family. Her father and Robert were already at the table, waiting to be served.

"What's going on out there?" You are sure spending a lot of time out in the backyard lately. Are you keeping some kind of animal out there?" asked her mother.

"I'll bet it's skunks," chided Robert.

"Yeah, I'm saving them for your next birthday so that you will have someone to play with," Jenny joked.

"Or maybe… she's harboring the vicious criminal who's been terrorizing the town," said Robert. Robert and Jenny began to verbally attack each other.

"Stop it, you two, I'm not going to warn you again," warned their father.

"Anyway mom, I'm really hungry this morning. Could I get a little extra?" begged Jenny.

"I suppose so," said her mother. Then her mother used up the last of the pancake batter. All the while that Jenny was at the breakfast table, she had a paper bag sitting on her lap beneath the tabletop. Occasionally some food found its way into the bag. After breakfast, the bag found its way to a hidden spot on the back porch until the coast was clear to go back and get it.

Jenny proceeded to do her Saturday chores as she normally would do, except that she kept watch on the shed as often as possible. But as Jenny carried the trash to the garbage cans by the garage, she spied Robert sneaking towards the shed.

Jenny couldn't yell at him at him as that would only make him go farther. She began to imagine all of the worst things that would happen to her. She prepared to accept her fate.

"Robert! Robert, come here! Your father is leaving for a convention today and I need to go downtown before he goes. I'm taking you there to get some new shoes. Turn around and let's go because we don't have much time to waste," said their mother, rather hurriedly.

"But mom… I want to see what Jenny is hiding in there," whined Robert.

"You heard me! We're going now!" his mother threatened. Defeated, Robert turned, then followed her to the car, snarling at Jenny all of the way. Before they got to the end of the driveway, Jenny was on the telephone with the others to explain what just occurred.

"Come quick, we don't have much time ourselves," said Jenny. Once they were all there, they gathered at the door to the shed.

"Are you still there?" asked Jenny.

"Yes, I am still here," said a voice from inside the door. Then the four stepped inside.

"We would like to ask you some questions," James said.

"You said that you were from another planet. How did you get here?" he asked.

"My spaceship," said the other Jenny.

"Why here and where is your spaceship?" asked James.

"One of my modules burned out in my control panel and this was the closest place to land," the alien said.

"We searched for you ship, but we could not find it," Gary said.

"It is buried in the sand dunes by the water," the alien said.

"Why are you here? Are you here to eat us or take over the planet?" asked Miles.

"Miles! Geez… what a question," they all cried. But Miles was only getting started.

"Do you have trees on your planet? Do you have clouds there? Do you have pets? Do you have a family?" pestered Miles. The last question seemed to make the alien sad.

"Way to go, guys. We'll help you whatever way we can. By the way, what did you say that your name was?" asked Jenny.

"How is it that you speak, Earthling?" asked Gary. He explained that all of Earth's broadcasts reached his planet so they learned all of Earth's languages.

"What did you say your name was again?" asked Jenny.

"You cannot say it," he explained.

"All right then I think we should call you… Ralph," said Jenny.

"My family will be back before too long, so we should stock up on some food and other supplies. My father keeps a kind of electronics lab in our basement because of his work, maybe there is something we could fix your ship with," Jenny offered. All of them went inside the house and headed for the basement. There they found tables loaded with all sorts of wires, motors, and switches. Ralph found some electronic boards that he examined closely.

"Maybe… ," was all that the alien would say.

"With my brother being such a snoop, I think you should sleep downstairs tonight, Ralph. Besides, it should be more comfortable for sleeping there than the drafty old shed. In the meantime, we need to find you another place to hide out in, and by the way, can you please, please, please, possibly make yourself look like someone else other than me? There is no way to explain how there could be two mes being in the same room," Jenny said.

"All right, but you all must turn around for a brief moment while I transform myself," explained the alien.

"Why?" asked James.

"Please do as I ask, or I will not transform. It will be only for a very short time. Now, ready… now turn." The gang did as asked, and they turned and faced away from him.

"You may look now." They turned back around, and to their complete surprise, there stood one of their classmates from school. It was a little disconcerting to see the kid standing before them. It was perfect except for the voice. It would seem that Ralph had seen him but not heard him speak. None of them spoke for a very long time. It was James who finally broke the silence.

"Hey Gary, how about we hide Ralph in your garage loft in the back?" Gary didn't want to commit himself, so he hesitated for a long time before he answered.

"Okay, but I need time to clear out a space for him. Maybe he can move in Sunday night." Then Jenny had an inspiration on her own.

"Next Thursday and Friday are parent conference days, right? The office will be busy with paperwork. Now, suppose Ralph could spend at least part of his day with us instead of having to hide himself day and night."

"Are you nuts? How could he possibly pull such a plan like that off?" James asked.

"Parents are always moving in or out of town. It's no big deal. So what if Miss Peachtree has a new student. Who really cares anyway?" protested Jenny.

"Ralph has travelled all those light years in a spacecraft with technologies that we can only imagine of. Why would he spend his time with a bunch of kids anyway? Wouldn't he be bored to death?" asked James.

"I'll do it!" cried the alien.

"Well, anyway, let's get Ralph settled in for the night, then we can move him over to Gary's tomorrow evening under the cover of darkness. Let's go into the kitchen and make Ralph's dinner," said Jenny.

They all followed Jenny into the kitchen. She reached into the cabinets and started to bring out various jars of food.

"I didn't know you could cook," said Gary.

"I can't, but at least I can make sandwiches, especially peanut butter and jelly sandwiches. Here let me finish this one up, Ralph, then take a bite and let me know if you like it," offered Jenny. Ralph took a small bite out of one of the corners.

"It is good, but may I add something to it?" he asked. There were some pickles already on the table and a bottle of hot sauce. He added both to the sandwich and took another bite. They grimaced as he swished it all around his mouth and swallowed it.

"How was it?" asked James.

"Better," was all that he said. He recognized the container of hot chocolate, so he asked if Jenny would make him some. She made it for Ralph, then poured it in a thermos bottle to keep it hot. Then he asked for some Halloween candy.

"Don't they have sugar on your planet?" asked James. Jenny heard a car door slam shut and she began to panic.

"Scatter, everybody! My parents are home. I'll see you tomorrow night. Ralph, come with me downstairs and lay low until I can come and get you," warned Jenny. They hurried off to the basement, carrying Ralph's dinner and a blanket so that he could sleep in comfort.

As Jenny re-emerged from below, she looked out of the kitchen window in time to see Robert head for the shed like a blood-hound following a scent.

"Have fun, twerp," jeered Jenny.

CHAPTER ELEVEN

Gary spent most of Sunday afternoon preparing Ralph's room. It was in the attic of the family's garage. It was the perfect hideout as it had running water and an electrical outlet into which he could plug in some kind of appliance. By nightfall it was ready. The next step was to sneak Ralph out of his basement hiding place and into his new temporary home. Gary called Jenny's house, pretending to ask about a homework assignment.

"I'll be there in a few minutes, get Ralph ready to go," he said. Then he hung up the telephone.

Jenny's family was watching their favorite television show and they planted themselves in their favorite spots. It was a good time to move Ralph.

"Does anybody want something from the kitchen?" asked Jenny. Fortunately, they all said no. Jenny went into the kitchen, then called softly to Ralph.

"Time to go, Ralph. Be as quiet as possible. Gary is here to take you to your new place," she whispered.

Jenny was both sad and happy to see Ralph go. The alien was almost discovered several times, and Robert was not making it easy for her to keep Ralph hidden.

The next few days were quiet as the fourth graders let everything cool down. Gary was the only one to visit Ralph, bringing him contraband food and goodies. He had even found an old radio and record player so that he might be able to amuse himself as long as he kept the volume and the lights dimmed.

On Wednesday night, Gary approached Ralph with a piece of paper with some written instructions.

"Tomorrow and Friday are the school conferences with the parents. Tomorrow would be the perfect time to get registered for our class. Here are the instructions to get there. Make sure that you appear as an adult and not as somebody who already lives in town. This is the address to use and other things to know. Just follow this list and, 10:00 will be when to go," said Gary. He gave Ralph some adult clothes and his dinner.

"See you tomorrow," Gary said.

Both Miles and Garry had their conferences in the morning. Miles went home, but Gary waited around for Jenny and James. A number of unfamiliar grown-ups roamed the school, but none of them could be recognized as perhaps as being Ralph.

"Has anybody seen him?" asked James. The rest merely shrugged their shoulders indicating that they weren't sure.

"I guess we can ask him on Saturday," said James. Then they returned home with their own parents.

On Saturday morning, Jenny ate breakfast with her family.

"I see that you're not spending so much time in the backyard lately," said Jenny's mother.

"No, I'm bored with that. After I do my regular chores, can I go over to Gary's?" asked Jenny.

At first, Jenny's mother was against the idea, but Jenny was persistent, wearing down her mother's resistance.

"Please, please, please. I know that the town is still scared, but the thefts have totally stopped and besides, I won't be alone."

"All right, but you have to be home by eight o'clock or else," warned her mother.

"Don't worry, I will be." At that she left for Gary's house.

A few minutes later, she was in Gary's house with the others questioning Ralph. They all asked if he were able to enroll in Miss Peachtree's class.

"I think so. I was told to stop by the office Monday morning," said the alien. They dropped the subject after that. Gary and the others spent the rest of their time together showing Ralph how to use the record player and how to find Ralph's favorite stations on the radio. James gave Ralph some of his old scientific magazines to look at. They were doing their level best to keep the alien's spirits afloat.

CHAPTER TWELVE

The mood was rather somber come Monday morning for James and the others when there was no new student in the classroom and they were sorely disappointed. However by the middle of the morning, the principal knocked softly on the door jamb to the classroom.

"Sorry for the interruption Miss Peachtree, but we have a new student joining us today.

"Please welcome Ernie to your class!" beamed the principal. James and Jenny looked at each other in utter disbelief as if to say "Oh no!". He had a small thin mouth and thick glasses. He was in fact the perfect target for the school bully.

"Please take a seat over by the window and we will get started on the next subject," said the teacher. Gary and the others kept looking at each other wondering if Ralph was able to pull off such a disguise. She handed Ralph a book so that he could follow along with the rest of the class. At the top of the hour, Miss Peachtree made an announcement.

"Put your books away in your desks, and bring out your science notebooks ," said the teacher.

Science! The mention of the word brought a smile to Ralph's face.

"Today we will discuss the topic of electricity. All of your homes should have it by now so please pay attention," said Miss Peachtree. She then placed a wooden frame on her desk with all sorts of switches and lights and other electrical doodads of sorts attached to it.

"Can any of you tell me how an electrical circuit works?" asked the teacher. None of the students ventured to give an answer. After an uncomfortable silence Ralph raised his hand to give an answer.

"It seems that our new student is the only one to dare to give an answer. Please go ahead let the rest of your fellow students how it works, said Miss Peachtree.

Then Ralph went into an amazing amount of detail about atoms and their structure. He then talked about orbital shells and other strange structures of atoms. He also talked about how atoms break up into positive and negative ions. After a while Miss Peachtree decided to rescue her students by politely interrupting Ralph.

"It seems that we are running out of time. Why don't we take a break and go to lunch a few minutes early?" Miss Peachtree offered. There were no objections from the other students.

"All right, beginning with the first row, you may line up and get your lunches from your locker if you brought your lunch from home. The rest of you may sit quietly until you are dismissed," said the teacher.

Unfortunately, Ralph had no lunch from home nor did he have any money to spend on a school lunch, but he joined the gang for lunch. They sat at a table that was located in the corner of the cafeteria so that they could talk in private away from the rest of the other students.

"Here Ralph, you can have one of my sandwiches," Jenny offered. She placed it on a clean napkin. She put it in front Ralph for him to eat. But Ralph just stared at it as if he were disappointed.

"What's the matter? Is there something wrong with the sandwich?" asked Jenny.

"I'd much prefer what you call Halloween candy. You wouldn't happen to have some, would you?" asked the alien.

"No, we don't Ralph," said Miles.

"That's all right, I will make use of what you have given me," said Ralph. He then grabbed a bottle of maple syrup that was still sitting on the table from breakfast and he poured it noisily over his sandwich.

Somehow, he managed to produce packet of hot sauce from somewhere and he added it to his sandwich. But before he could put it into his mouth, there was a great deal of commotion from one of the other tables.

It was George, who was also known as the school bully, collecting lunch money from the other frightened students.

"Maybe if we ignore him, he will go away," said Miles hopefully. But just as soon as Miles finished his sentence, George came dancing over to their table.

"Well, what do we have here? "Who's the new twerp?" demanded George.

"Ah leave him alone, he's new to our school," said Jenny.

"I'll give him until tomorrow, but for the rest of you, hand over your money," the bully threatened. James and the others handed over their dimes.

"Okay loser, I see that you made a sandwich especially for me," said George. He yanked the sandwich from Ralph's hands and then crammed it all into his mouth. He started to dance around furiously and began screaming.

"You tried to poison me! I'll be waiting for you after school," threatened the bully. He ran off to clean his mouth out with water.

"You had better watch out for him Ralph, he means to do you some serious harm. Maybe you could appear as somebody else," said Miles.

"Don't worry about me. Why did the other students give him their money?" asked Ralph.

"They didn't give it to him, he took it," explained James. Then went on to explain how a bully operates.

"I see," mused Ralph. Instead of going out to the playground after eating their lunch, they went to the classroom instead. They were uneasy for the rest of that day. They feared for Ralph's safety.

When the dismissal bell rang, they filed their way down the stairway to the front of the building.

From there they could see that George was waiting for them to come out. Gary and the rest made their way to the swings where they could watch everything from there. They waited for what seemed an eternity, but nothing happened.

The next morning all of the students were at their desks as if nothing ever happened. Ernie acted as if everything was as it normally was. James and the others waited until lunch to talk to Ralph.

"All right tell us what really happened," demanded Jenny.

"Nothing, nothing at all," answered Ralph. They tried to question him further, but they saw George making his way over to their table and they braced themselves for whatever might happen. It looked as if George had already eaten and was on his way to the playground.

"Hand over your money twerp," demanded George. They all handed over their money to George. As they did so Ralph edged his chair closer to George's side. The bully put his hand in his pocket to put away the money. It was very quiet for a short while. Then George began to dance around in crazy circles.

"Ow! Ow, ow make it stop!" yelled George.

"Ralph, what did you do to him?" cried James.

"Nothing that will hurt him. I feel like some fresh air," said Ralph. After the bully was out of sight, they began to talk excitedly amongst themselves.

Suddenly Jenny tried to break the tension by blurting out a sudden inspiration that had just come to her.

"I have an idea Ralph, why don't you come over to my house for Thanksgiving dinner? It will be a chance for you to see something other than the school and give you chance to get out of your hiding place," offered Jenny. But Ralph seemed a little hesitant.

"It will also be an opportunity to check out my father's basement. Remember, my father has a workshop down there. Maybe you can find something to fix your ship with," said Jenny further. That was music to the alien's ears. He began to miss his family terribly.

"I'll say that you are some sort of exchange student and that you have no one to celebrate the holiday with. I'm sure that it will be okay with my parents." Ralph agreed to come as he had nothing to lose.

"Hey guys, if Ralph makes it till the end of the week, how about we take him to our favorite shop for a treat?" asked Gary. Even Miles who doesn't get excited about very much thought it might be fun. There was no sign of George until the next day.

It was then that Miss Peachtree angrily addressed her class.

"I have been getting reports that students from this class have been picking on George from Miss Gordan's class. If I hear that any one of you are doing such a thing, he or she will be sent immediately to the principal's office. Get your things and behave yourselves," Miss Peachtree warned. The dismissal bell rang and the students headed off for lunch.

James and the gang found their usual table and sat down to eat.

"Can you believe that! We are picking on George?! NOW I've heard everything," growled Jenny.

"Cool it, speaking of the devil, look who is headed straight for our table, said Gary. George took great strides on his way to their table. At first, George just stood there. Then he pointed his finger at them accusingly in poor Ralphs face.

"You and me, after school, behind the building. And you had better show your face," demanded George. Then he stomped off.

"You're not really going to do it are you, Ralph?" asked a worried Miles.

"Why yes of course," said Ralph as if it wasn't a big deal. The rest of the day Ralph showed no signs of being worried whatsoever.

When it was time to resume class, they waited for Miss Peachtree to let them have it, but instead she had a surprise announcement for them.

"The office has informed us that our math sessions will be different for the rest of the school year. We will be given a comprehensive exam soon to test our knowledge of math principles," explained the teacher. The whole class let out a terrible groan.

"I also need to mention that it will account for half of this term's grade," explained the teacher. The class let out an even bigger groan. They felt that it would be better to be sent to the principal's office.

The rest of the day dragged on as they waited for the dismissal bell to ring. When it did, they rushed off to give Ralph their moral support. Unfortunately, Jenny's and Gary's mothers were waiting to pick them up.

At least James and Gary were able to stay and watch. Ralph finally showed and a crowd began to form around him.

The teachers began to sense that something was to happen so they shooed the students away.

"You know that you are not allowed to be here after school is dismissed. Until the streets are safe again you have to go home," said Miss Wolf the sixth-grade teacher.

But Ralph managed to slip away unnoticed with all of the chaos going on. With any luck, either Gary or James might see what would happen. Otherwise, they would have to wait until morning for any news.

CHAPTER THIRTEEN

The next morning, the class started as any other. Miss Peachtree took attendance as she normally did. And there sitting at his desk was Ernie acting as if nothing ever happened. Gary was able to sneak away and ask Ralph about the night before. But the alien was not very helpful with any answers. Even then he only gave one-word replies.

What did George do to you Ralph?" asked Jenny

"Nothing."

"Something had to have happened," said James.

When at lunch it seemed that they would get any answers, they saw George heading straight for their table.

"Brace yourselves," warned Miles. But what happened next was something that they would have never imagined, except of course for Ralph.

George threw a handful of dimes on their table.

"This is what I took last week, I'm sorry," apologized the bully. Then George walked off without saying another word.

"What just happened?" said an unbelieving Miles.

"Ralph, did you threaten George or take over his mind?" asked Miles.

"I did no such thing, we just came to an agreement, that's all," replied Ralph.

"That must have been some kind of understanding! Oh, by the way, Ralph my parents said that it was okay for you to come over for Thanksgiving with us. And while you're there maybe we can check out my dad's workshop for something you can use to fix your ship with." A small smile broke over Ralph's face. It wasn't much, but at least there was a glimmer of hope.

"Say, didn't we promise Ralph that we would take him to our favorite store and get some of our favorite snacks?" asked James.

"Good idea, and while we're stuffing our faces, we could teach Ralph the finer points of eating with a knife and a fork," said Gary.

They finished their lunch as quickly as they could in order to spend more time on the playground. They were amazed to see George getting off of his swing and offering it to a second grader.

"Now we know that Ralph did something to him, this just doesn't feel right," said Miles. The bell rang again and they all went back to class. It was a long day for them. They only wanted to go home to start the weekend.

Unfortunately, Miss Peachtree was about to put another damper on their plans.

"Before I dismiss you, I should remind you about the upcoming exam next week. I want you to study extra hard over the break," she said

"AWWW!" whined the entire class.

As the final bell rang out, the students jockeyed themselves so that they would be the first to get through the classroom door. The gang rushed for their bikes that were waiting for them on the bike racks. When they got there, they noticed a problem. That problem was that there were five riders, but only four bikes. Miles was the bigger and the stronger of the group so he was chosen to put Ralph on his bike. Miles waited for Ralph to hop on the back of his bike. When he had done so, he started peddling as hard as he could. To his surprise, he found that the alien weighed very little.

It wasn't very long before they came to the little store. They laid down their bikes carefully along the curb. They entered the shop together. Immediately, Ralph spotted the candy counter and he placed his face right up to the glass front. An unhappy storeowner gave them a warning.

"Your buddy is scaring me. Have him pick something and take him outside will you please," he said. But Ralph wanted it all.

"Ralph remember that we only have just so much to work with. So pick something you might like and we'll get it for you. Go ahead and get something," said James.

After paying for their snacks, the gang sat out on the curb with Ralph. He ate some of the candy that he chose and they watched him. Jenny tried to explain the finer points on how to eat properly. Then she gave him the details for the visit to her house.

The next day was Thanksgiving and the weather forecast was for light flurries, but the day started out warm and dry. It promised to be a good day for a holiday.

Ralph had to be gone from Gary's place by ten o'clock because his relatives were to show up then. Jenny's mother wasn't going to serve dinner until noon, so he showed a couple of hours early.

At ten o'clock right on the nose, Ralph climbed the steps to Jenny's front porch and rang the doorbell.

"Jenny, your friend is here, my hands are full, let him in, will you?" asked her mother.

"All right, I'll get it," said Jenny. Then she went out to the front porch to talk with Ralph.

"Remember what we told you, your name is Howard, and you are from a small county in central Europe. When replying to my father, say 'yes sir,' and when replying to my mother, say 'yes ma'am,' then they will know that you are not from around here. Oh, and one more thing, don't get into any arguments with my bratty brother, Robert, for any reason. Just follow my lead and you'll be fine." Then they went inside to meet the rest of the family who were waiting to be introduced to Howard the exchange student.

"Um, everyone this is Howard from school."

"How come I never seen him before?" jeered Robert.

"Robert, please!" cried Jenny's mother.

"Well, dinner is still cooking. Jenny maybe you can take Howard into the living room to watch some football with the rest of the family," she said.

Jenny escorted Ralph to a stuffed chair in the corner of the living room. Robert came skipping in shortly after and he planted himself in a chair directly across from Ralph, from which he stared rudely at Ralph, making the atmosphere a little uncomfortable.

Jenny's dad came in next and sat down to watch the game. He sensed that something was a bit off, so he tried to start a conversation with Howard.

"Do you have anything like our football where you come from, Howard?" he asked.

"No, but we play a sport that involves a metal ball and some charged wands. A small hoop is suspended in mid-air. The contestants then charge their wands to either a positive or a negative charge, then they try to push the metal ball through the hoop. Whoever is able to get the ball into the hoop first before the others wins that round."

"Um, " was all that Jenny's dad could think to say. Jenny saw Robert making circles with his fingers, pointed at his temple.

"I think that I'll grab a football and play catch with Howard for a while," said an embarrassed Jenny. Jenny found a football, then took Ralph outside to kill some time before dinner.

"Try to catch it, Howard, here it comes," said Jenny. She threw the football directly at Ralph. He just stood there , and the ball bounced limply off Ralph's stomach and hit the ground. Jenny looked around, hoping that nobody had seen what just occurred.

"Look, we have a little time left before we eat. Let's go down to my dad's workshop and get what you need to repair your ship," Jenny said. They entered through the back cellar door. Jenny switched on a small, weak light and they gathered up some things.

"Won't your dad miss some of these things?" asked Ralph.

"If I have to use some of my allowance, I will replace what we take," Jenny said. She found an old bookbag of hers, and she put everything inside and hid it in a corner. Afterwards, they just sat on the front steps and waited for the meal.

"Robert, did you see where Howard and Jenny went? It's time to eat, so invite them in," said Jenny's mother. Robert did so, but he seemed a little too happy to do so.

"It's time to eat, you lovebirds. Make sure that you bring your boyfriend," cackled Robert.

"How would you like to not see your next birthday?" threatened Jenny. They went inside for their Thanksgiving meal.

There was a place waiting for Ralph at the end of the table where everybody could see him.

"Before we dig in, let's go around the table and tell everyone what we are thankful for," said the father. Robert was thankful that this was the beginning of the main holiday season. Both parents were glad that they were all together. But Ralph appeared a little sad.

"What are you grateful for, Howard?" asked Jenny's mother.

"I miss my family. But I'm grateful for the friends that I have made here," said Ralph.

"I'm also grateful that my ship didn't break up upon landing," Ralph gratefully added. Jenny's mother's face grew most serious. Jenny decided to jump in before the conversation could go any further.

"I think he means that he was glad that his ship that he came on didn't break up before reaching the shore. Maybe there was a storm then or something," explained Jenny.

"Well anyway, we're glad you're safe and able to join us for the holiday celebration. Let's eat," said Jenny's father.

Ralph's eves glazed over when he noticed the pumpkin pie, the whipped cream, the candied yams and other sugary goodies. Jenny saw what Ralph was thinking and she wagged a finger at him, warning him to behave himself.

"That's for dessert, Howard. Ummm… apparently where Howard comes from, they eat their dessert first," Jenny offered.

"How quaint. Where did you say that you came from?" asked her mother.

"Probably one of those teeny backward jobs in Europe," chided Robert.

"Robert! Behave yourself!" Jenny's father demanded.

"Yeah, Robert. Let's just eat," said Jenny. Then Ralph started for the mashed potatoes. Jenny grabbed his hand and handed him a spoon so that he wouldn't scoop it out with his hands. Ralph placed a mound of potatoes on his plate. Then they heaped a pile of yams upon them. Then he heaped some turkey on that, then he added cranberries on that.

"Ooh, pickles!" then Ralph added that to his pile. When he had finished that, he poured gravy all over it to top it all off. Jenny's family tried their very best to try and not notice and they went on with the meal.

Somehow, they all got through the meal and dessert without any major problems. Any conversation after that was short and to the point, so as not to get into anything too embarrassing.

"It's getting late. Howard should be heading home now. I'll show him the way and then I will help with the dishes," Jenny said. She walked him to the front yard gate.

"The weather forecast for Sunday night is for snow, I think that it would be a good time to fix your spaceship because there would not be a lot of people walking around, and also if the snow is heavy enough, it might hide us from view. I'll let the others know so that we can be there in case someone comes by," she said. Jenny let Ralph through the gate, then watched him until he was out of sight.

She went inside to help with the dishes. As she dried, her mother surprised her.

"Oh, I almost forgot. Jill's mother called me earlier this afternoon and she invited the entire class to Jill's birthday party."

"No way. She thinks that I'm a loser. I don't wanna go," griped Jenny.

"You are going and that's final," said her mother.

"Mom?"

"We'll go shopping for a gift and you are bringing it to the party. No more backtalk," said Jenny's mother.

CHATER FOURTEEN

It was indeed snowy that day. In fact, it was almost too snowy. Jenny found herself rapping on Ralph's apartment door.

"We're ready to go, if you are. I brought along some tools in case we might need them." Jenny offered. After a short pause, Ralph came to the door, looking like Howard. He was at least dressed correctly for the weather.

"We told our parents that we are working on a class science project. It will be dark soon, so we had better get moving," said James. They grabbed their things and headed for the sand dune that hid Ralph's ship.

Once they found the right dune, they removed the snow covering it.

"Stand back please," said Ralph. He dug in his pockets until he found something that looked like a television remote. Ralph pushed a button, then the sand covering the ship began to fall away. A panel on the side of the ship slowly opened outward, then upward. A light shone upon what seemed to be a control console.

"Go inside, Ralph, and we will stand guard in case somebody comes by, although I don't think anyone will come out here on a night like this," said James.

They stood in the cold and blowing snow, while Ralph struggled with making the handmade parts fit his control console. Miles was of course the first to get bored and complain.

"How much longer, Ralph? I would like to go home and warm up," whined Miles.

"Cut him slack. Ralph isn't out here just for the fun of it, and neither are we," said Gary.

Ralph finally emerged from the ship.

"Stand back. If this works, I will be able to go home," he said. He took out his remote and pushed some more buttons. This time, the console began humming, then rows of lights came to life. Ralph looked really happy for the first time that they had known him.

But suddenly, a black cloud of smoke appeared. The lights dimmed, then died out. There was the terrible smell of burnt wiring. Ralph's face fell. Nobody said a word because they didn't know what to say.

"What happened, Ralph?" asked James.

"The components were not strong enough to hold. I will have to try another time," said the very disappointed alien.

"We will help in any way we can!" Gary offered. Ralph pushed a button on his remote, then the panel closed back up. They covered the ship with some loose sand.

"Let's go home before somebody spots us," said Jenny and they started back home.

Miles and Gary walked ahead of the rest. Then Jenny had another inspiration

"Know what, James?" asked Jenny.

"No, what?" he said.

"Since Ralph will be with us a little longer, maybe I can talk him into doing me a favor. After all, I provided a place for him until we found a better place to hide him. And I'm providing new parts for his spaceship," asked Jenny.

"What do you have in mind?" asked James.

"My mom is forcing me to go to Jill's birthday party. I really don't want to go. So… with the proper clothes and a little coaching, he can go in my place. Nobody would be able to tell us apart," Jenny said.

"Do you think that he would actually go for it?" asked James.

"He owes me after all that I did for him, how could he refuse?" she asked.

They were quiet for the walk home, but instead of going directly home, she went over to Ralph's. Once she felt he was alone, she knocked on his door. When he opened the door, he was surprised to see Jenny standing there. He asked her inside.

"What is it that you want from me?" asked the alien. Jenny explained the whole situation to him.

"What do you say, Ralph, will you do it?"

"I do not agree that it would be a very good idea. We should each learn how to deal with problems on our own as much as we are able to. Sometimes we might need help, but that is all right," Ralph said.

"Please Ralph, haven't I helped you along so far? It's only fair. Besides, I'm only asking you to attend a party in my place. That's it. I would do it for you if our positions were reversed," pleaded Jenny.

"Very well, but that will be the last time that I would do such a thing," he said.

"I will bring some clothes over and the gift to give the host, and we will go over some things you should know," said Jenny. At that Jenny left for home and Ralph prepared himself for bed.

Later that night, James was lying in bed, thinking over what Jenny told him. If Ralph agreed to do a favor for Jenny, how could he refuse to do one for him? What he had in mind was to have Ralph take his place for the math quiz.

James was in no way having trouble in math. In fact, he was doing quite well for himself. But James thought that Ralph, having such advanced scientific abilities, would make himself look like a math genius. Ralph would be sure to earn him an A+++.

Not only that, but James would be able to skate his way through to the end and still get a better than average grade. All he would need to do would be to provide Howard with an excuse slip explaining why he was absent that day so Ralph could take his place. Since Miles and Gary had no idea of what Jenny and James were planning, it wasn't part of their lunch talk. Instead, they talked about how they would help Ralph fix his ship so that he could get back home.

"Ralph, do you know what went wrong?" Gary asked.

"I do. I just need to find a way to make my repairs stronger somehow."

"Maybe we could visit my dad's shop again and get some more parts," Jenny offered.

As they were finishing their meal, they saw George storming down the aisle straight towards them.

"I knew it was too good to be true to last, " moaned Miles. They braced themselves, but George just blew on by. He stopped at a nearby table and picked a backpack that he must have forgotten. He then walked over to their table and apologized. "I'm sorry for bothering you. Have a good lunch," said the former bully.

"Ralph! What did you do to him? He was the meanest person we ever saw. Did you hypnotize him?" asked Jenny.

"No, George was replaced with another alien being. Or maybe, Ralph put an alien bug in George's brain. What did you do to George anyway?" asked Miles.

"We merely came to an understanding," said Ralph.

There were other surprises coming that day.

Miss Peachtree announced a contest that involved the entire school. All of the students would sell various kinds of candy bars. Whichever class sold the most bars would take a trip to the state capital for a day. The class started buzzing with excitement.

"Piece of cake. I plan on making that trip. Now, if we can keep Howard from eating the merchandise, we'll be a shoe in," said Jenny to a boy sitting next to her. He gave Jenny the strangest look because he didn't understand the inside joke.

"We also have the name of the school's student of the month," Miss Peachtree announced.

"Yeah, yeah, just say Louise Pringle like you always do," said Gary to himself as he rolled his eyes.

Miss Peachtree said, "This person is worthy of the title because that person has shown the most improvement in not only his or her schoolwork, but also with a vast improvement in his or her attitude in respecting other students."

Nobody was actually paying attention being it was so late in the day. They all just wanted to go home.

"And that person who has shown such remarkable personal improvement is… George Rittenberg," announced Miss Peachtree.

There was a stunned silence when Miss Peachtree read George's name aloud. They didn't know if they heard right. It had to be some sort of mistake. Did she really say George? 'The George,' the school bully. Next, to top it all off, she reminded the class of the impending math exam.

"Before we go, I want to remind all of you to study hard for the math exam this Friday. What I have decided to do is to give the test in the morning, then hold our holiday party that afternoon," said Miss Peachtree. Then the dismissal bell rang.

"Study hard now!" she said. James, who had no intention of studying hard, found Ralph on the way out.

"I will take you to the convenience store and buy you all the candy you want if you take the math exam for me," said James.

"That can't be right. How will your teacher measure how much you have learned in class? I am not comfortable with that. You should take your own test," said Ralph.

"I heard what you are doing for Jenny. I think it is only fair," said James.

James and Ralph argued back and forth until Ralph finally caved in.

CHAPTER FIFTEEN

The morning of that fateful test was unusually cold and gray, but that mattered very little to James. When he came down for breakfast, he was more cheerful than usual.

"I have never seen anyone so happy to take a test before," said his mother.

"It will be a good day." Then James finished his cereal and grabbed his backpack, which seemed heavier and more stuffed than normal. It was daylight out, so James had snuck out to avoid being noticed that he was headed for Gary's garage.

Ralph, or rather, James, was already waiting for him. James changed out of his clothes then gave them to Ralph to wear to class. James asked Ralph if he had any questions for him which he didn't.

"You had better go, Ralph, it's getting late." Ralph did not look very happy as he was leaving but he didn't say another word.

Ralph was barely out the door when James pulled out some snacks that he would eat throughout the day. After that he pulled out some of his favorite magazine and comic books and placed them next to the chair. Lastly, he took out some records for Ralph's record player that he had borrowed. Then a huge grin drew across his face as James placed his legs atop Ralph's coffee table.

"I'm going to be famous." Then he smiled some more.

At school, Miss Peachtree took attendance for the classroom. She noticed a note for Ernie. Without further delay, she passed out the test while giving out instructions on how to fill out the exam.

"The test is in sections, so when you finish the section that you are working on, turn your paper over and put your pencil down and I will come and pick it up. If you finish before I say stop, just sit quietly while we wait for the others to finish. When I say now, you may begin. Good luck, fourth graders, you may begin now."

There was a great rustling of papers and a great scritch-scratching of pencils. To Miss Peachtree's amazement, James put down his pencil then folded his hands on top of his desk. Luckily the other students were too busy to notice.

"Time! Put your pencils down and we will take a break before we continue with the next section. Get a drink of water or whatever you need, but do not bother any of the other classes please," said Miss Peachtree.

Jenny and Gary met at the water fountain so they could compare notes.

"Did you see how fast James finished his paper?" There will be no living with him, not that it's so great now," Gary said. Jenny, who knew that it was really Ralph taking the test, had to agree.

"Let's go back before we get into trouble," Jenny said. The class found their seats once again and waited for the word to start the second section of the test.

"Bring out the packet marked number two. All right, ready, begin now," the teacher said. The students began furiously marking their papers. Once again, Ralph in the guise of James, tore his way through the test and put his pencil down before many of the others started. This time Miss Peachtree barely lifted her eyes from her own papers.

This happened two more times before the teacher called an end to the exam.

"Let's break for lunch. We will take it easy this afternoon so we will use the last hour for our party," Miss Peachtree said. Then Miss Peachtree led the students to the cafeteria for lunch.

Neither Gary nor Miles cared to bring up the topic of the test. Ralph was not very talkative either. Instead he brought out the lunch that James' parents had packed for James and began to eat. As they all sat there, George came running towards them.

"It looks like George is going to rescue Timmy from the well again," joked Jenny. She was encouraged by the fact that the plan was working out so wonderfully for James. Nobody noticed the difference between Ralph and the real James. Ralph should be able to pull off her plan with such ease.

It was hard to wait for the party to begin. As the class was allowed free time to read whatever they pleased, Miss Peachtree set up a long table in the back and began to load it up with treats of every kind. It did not escape Ralph's notice. There were treats that even the convenience store hadn't stocked.

Jenny noticed the hungry look in Ralph's eyes. She wagged a finger at him as if to say 'No, Ralph.' Ralph seemed to understand. He restrained himself until it was time for the party to begin. He was able to behave himself and he actually had a wonderful time. Ralph was able to take home some of the leftovers.

On the way home, Jenny and Ralph had a long discussion about how families got together and celebrated the holiday season. It made Ralph quite sad.

"Don't worry, Ralph, we'll get you back home some way or another. Don't forget that you are taking my place at Jill's party tomorrow. All I'm asking you to do is to enjoy yourself like you did today. Come over to my house an hour before the party starts and I will let you into my dad's shop so that you can figure out what you may need to repair your spaceship," Jenny said.

Ralph looked a little sad still.

"You have my word, Ralph, just wait, you'll get home again," promised Jenny.

CHAPTER SIXTEEN

It was about one o'clock in the afternoon on Saturday, when there was a knock on Jenny's front door.

"Jenny, your friend Howard is at the front door. Come down and talk to him," said Jenny's mother. She came running down the stairs with a backpack in each hand.

"What are you going to do with those bags?" asked her mother.

"One is for carrying Jill's birthday present and the other is for some extra clothes in case I spill on myself," explained Jenny. Then she opened one bag to reveal that there was indeed a different set of clothes inside of it. Her mother was wondering why all of a sudden Jenny, who was the neighborhood tomboy should suddenly be concerned about her clothes. She had better things to think about so she let it slide for the time being.

"Could we please go downstairs for a little bit before we head out for Jill's party?!" asked Jenny.

"Fine, but don't be too long," said her mother. Then both Ralph and Jenny descended the steps into the basement. Ralph gathered up the things that he thought useful for the repair of his ship. He gave them to Jenny who placed them beneath the clothes in one of the bags. "Let's go back to your room and get you changed into another set of clothes. She handed Ralph the clothes that she would be wearing to the party and went and changed into them. He emerged, looking exactly like Jenny herself. She stood there looking directly at him, wondering if that is what she really appeared as.

"Relax, Ralph. Give this to whatever adult greets you and do whatever they ask you to do. And don't eat anything until everyone else does," said Jenny. She handed Jill's gift to Ralph and sent him on his way with instructions on how to find Jill's house.

Once the phony Jenny was on her way the real Jenny made herself comfortable in Ralph's room. She put on some of her favorite music, then she put up her feet on Ralph's coffee table. Ralph's room has actually quite comfortable, despite the fact a gentle snow began to fall outside. Jenny sat back in her chair with a huge grin on her face. Then she cracked open her favorite soda to celebrate.

The party was scheduled to end by two o'clock, but when it got to be four, there was no sign of Ralph. Even if he had to walk home, that was plenty of time for him to be back. Another half hour went by, and Ralph still hadn't gotten home. Jenny started to panic, fearing something had gone terribly wrong. Just as Jenny was preparing to go find him, Ralph gently rapped on his door to let Jenny know that he was home. After Ralph was safely inside, Jenny practically pounced on him." What are you so late? Did something go wrong? Did someone discover that you weren't really me?" asked a panicky Jenny.

"It was fine. Want some cake? I have plenty left over," offered Ralph. Then he showed her a box containing what looked to be half of a sheet cake.

"Where on Earth did you get all that cake, Ralph? Never mind, don't answer that, I'm not sure that I want to know. Now that you're here, I will give you the items you picked form my dad's workshop that I had hidden. Unless you let us know, the gang is planning on coming over just as soon as it gets dark. I'll let you get started on your repairs. I better get going because my parents are probably freaking out. Thank you for helping me out. That will be the last favor I ask of you, goodbye," said Jenny. She put on her coat, then left for home.

Jenny's mother met her at the front door.

"Where were you, young lady? I was worried sick. There wasn't some kind of trouble, was there?" asked her mother.

"I did my duty and now I'm home," said an impatient Jenny.

"How was the party? Did Jill like her present? Did everyone have a good time?"

"Mom! Please! Everyone had a good time, Jill liked her gift, and we ate cake."

"Well, dinner will be ready soon if you're still hungry After we eat, we can watch a holiday movie on television."

They all had a nice family meal, after which they all pitched in and did the dishes. Jenny popped some popcorn, then the family went into the living room to watch their holiday show on television.

As Jenny sat in front of the flickering television screen, a smile drew across her face as she recalled the events of that day. "He did it! He really did it! Too bad he has to go home. There would be a real market for Ralph's talents. But I don't want to keep him from his family."

CHAPTER SEVENTEEN

"Psst, hey Ralph, are you ready? Let's get going. None of us wants to get into any trouble. My parents think that I'm in my bedroom reading a book," said Gary.

Ralph came out carrying a bag of electronics with which he hoped would get him home.

"Maybe this time you would be able to take off. We'll miss you, Ralph."

They had no trouble reaching the disabled spaceship. Gary and James stood gaurd while Jenny and Miles assisted Ralph. Ralph reached into his pocket and retrieved his remote for the ship. He pushed the button that allowed Ralph access to the ship. They watched as the sand shifted and the side panel opened silently.

Jenny and Miles waited patiently as Ralph went to work on the ship. It seemed as torture as poor Ralph struggled for a seeming eternity to complete his repairs.

"I am finished. I need for you to stand back in case something would go wrong," said the alien. He held his remote in his right hand and pushed a red colored button.

From inside the spaceship came a low hum. Light after light and row after row of lights blinked to life.

"You did it Ralph!" they cried. But then…

Poof! Gray smoke poured out of the ship's interior.

"What happened, Ralph?" asked James. But Ralph gave no answer. Instead, he just stood there, staring into space.

After a long silence, Ralph spoke out.

"Your technology is not advanced enough to make the repairs permanent to travel on into space. I don't know how I will make it back home," moaned the alien.

"Don't give up quite yet. My father is always coming home with new gadgets, especially the kind that I don't understand," consoled Jenny. It was a quiet walk back home that night. The children were sad for Ralph, but they were also glad that they were still with them.

None of them slept very well that night, but what was to be done? They also realized that they would not hide Ralph forever. If he was to be discovered, they would probably never be allowed to speak to him again.

The students from the school were nonetheless enjoying the vacation from their studies, and Jenny enjoyed hers also. That was, until she and her mother began talking at the breakfast table.

"After you went to bed last night, I received a phone call from Jill's mother," said her mother. Jenny suddenly got a frightened look on her face. "Relax, it was nothing bad. In fact, it was something good," said her mother.

"Well, what then? If I didn't do anything wrong, why would Jill's mother be calling you at home?" Jenny asked.

"It seems that you were the life of the party; in fact, so much so that you are invited to another party," said her mother.

"And whose party would that be?!" snorted Jenny. "I think that it was someone named Kenny D," said her mother.

"No freaking way!" gasped Jenny. She had a crush on Kenny as long as she could remember.

"Yes, way. Or was it Kenny B? That's it, now I remember, it was Kenny B." Jenny avoided Kenny B ever since first grade because she thought he was kind of creepy.

"Nope, not goin'," protested Jenny.

"They were kind enough to invite you over. I told them that you are going, so you are going." Jenny felt that she was trapped into going. She was the one who made Ralph take her place at the party. She had no way to know what happened at Jill's house. She couldn't' risk exposing Ralph or herself for that matter. She knew that it was fruitless to argue.

Robert, her brother, had been listening behind the kitchen came waltzing into the room taunting Jenny.

"Jenny and Kenny B, sitting in a tree K-I-S-S-I-N-G." Jenny formed a tightly clenched fist.

"How about you kiss this, Robert?" she threatened. Robert then hid himself behind their mother.

"She's going to beat me up!" Robert yelped.

"Stop it, the both of you, right now or else!" warned their mother.

"Jill's mother also told me about the contest to sell the most chocolate in order to win a class trip. While she was at the school picking up Jill's candy, she also picked up yours. She will be here shortly so that you can get started on selling it right away."

"Can this day get any worse?" moaned Jenny.

The tension was broken when the telephone rang. Robert ran off to answer it.

"Mom, it's for you, it's Dad calling all the way from Boston." She ran off as quickly as possible to see what the matter was. She came back into the kitchen with a big smile upon her face.

"Good news! Your father is coming home early from his trip so that he can spend the holidays with the family. It was on the condition that he test out some inventions in his shop. Isn't that great?" asked their mother.

It was indeed good news. Maybe her dad would let Ralph, disguised as Howard, work alongside of him in his lab. Besides, who knows, it might be possible that Ralph might help her dad come up with some new fantastic invention of their own.

But as for celebrating the actual holidays, Jenny figured that it was somebody else's turn to entertain the alien. After she had dinner, Jenny went straight up to her room; she wasn't interested in watching any shows on television.

After a good night's sleep, Jenny decided to give Ralph the good news. She decided to kill two birds with one stone. If she had to go out and sell candy door to door, she might as well have some company with her.

"Mom, I think that I will go out and try to sell my candy. I don't know what time that I will be back, but I should be home for dinner," Jenny said.

"It's too dangerous for you to go out by yourself, young lady."

"But I won't be by myself, I'm going with Howard."

"Well, okay, if you don't be out long, be back for dinner." Jenny grabbed some of her candy and walked over to Gary's house so that she could talk to Ralph. Gary's family was not at home, which made things a little easier. It wouldn't look right for three of them to peddle their candy at the same time, as many people would find it too intimidating.

Jenny gently knocked on Ralph's door, being careful not to be heard. It took a while, but Ralph finally answered the door. He swung the door wide open without first asking who it was.

"You really should ask who is knocking before opening the door, Ralph," warned Jenny.

"Sorry, who is it?"

"Never mind, I have two things to talk to you about. The first thing I want to tell you is that my father is coming home early so that he will be spending the holiday with us. The reason is so that he can work on some new projects. Maybe there will be something new with which to fix your spaceship," said Jenny. She thought that what she said would make Ralph happy, but it only made him sad.

"Aw, cheer up, Ralph, you already proved that you can fix your ship. You just need the right materials. We'll work it out so that you can get to my dad's workshop." Ralph seemed a little gladder and more hopeful with Jenny's words.

"The other thing is that I want to know if you want to go with me as I sell my boxes of candy. I have them sitting outside your door. Maybe I will let you sell some too," offered Jenny.

"I have already sold all of mine," said Ralph.

"How could you Ralph? This is the first time I would've gone out," groaned Jenny. At first, she thought he was fibbing.

"Did you eat it all? Show me the money you collected," demanded Jenny. Ralph reached behind an old easy chair in his room and produced a pouch containing a neat stack of dollar bills and some change.

"Will this make you believe me?" asked Ralph. Jenny became a bit red in her face.

"How did you do it, Ralph? Did you hypnotize them or something?" asked Jenny.

"I did no such thing! I would not force anybody into doing something that they would not normally do," said a very insulted alien.

"I'm sorry, Ralph. I should not have accused you of something without knowing all of the facts. I haven't sold anything yet. If you could forgive me, I would like to ask you to go along with me as I try to sell my candy. Maybe you can give me a few tips as we go along," Jenny said.

Jenny timidly handed Ralph his winter jacket which he put on, and together they went off to sell some candy. Along the way, she asked him if he had heard of something called a transistor.

"Do you think that it could be something you use to fix your ship with?" Ralph suddenly became deep in thought.

"I will try to come up with some kind of excuse for you so that you can visit our house. Maybe then you can take a sneak peak at one of those transistors without raising any suspicions. I'll let you know what I come up with. You know, since you are stuck here, and there is time before school starts up again, maybe we should show you how we have fun during the winter season."

They did just that. The gang took him on a ride on a toboggan sledding some steep hillsides. They showed Ralph how to make a snow fort and how to lob snowballs at enemy positions. But Ralph really enjoyed himself when he was shown seasonal treats and goodies. He was given peppermint sticks, snickerdoodle cookies, eggnog and other sweets. That was something that Ralph could really get into but all good things must come to an end, so did winter break.

CHAPTER EIGHTEEN

In the meantime, Jenny's father came home and locked himself in his basement lab. Whatever it was that he was working on must have been really special. She would have to come up with a better idea. She promised Ralph and she vowed to carry through with it.

On the first day back at school, the whole class was suffering from holiday hang-over. There was also much anxiety over the test scores from before the break. It must have been an important test, because Miss Peachtree handed the test results to each student individually. But for whatever reason, she waited to give James his paper last. James was not at all concerned; in fact, he could barely wait.

"Here it comes, my A+ + +," he crowed to himself. But the scores were sealed to prevent the students from comparing their grades with each other.

As the teacher handed James his envelope, she told him, "Have your parents call me." Where were the hurrahs and all the congratulations? Still, James was not worried.

James ran home as fast as he could. He found both of his parents sitting at the kitchen table talking. He practically threw the envelope at them. His father carefully unsealed the test score and read the last page that gave the total score tally. His jaw seemed to drop open suddenly.

"James, you had better look at this," he said. He handed James his grade. It was bigger than life itself. It was an F. It was not just an F; it was printed with red ink and triple underlined! Before James could defend himself, his mother began to bawl him out.

"Miss Peachtree and I had a very interesting conversation. She was very disappointed in you. She said that you were much more capable than that. She very generously offered to allow you to bring your grade up by handing in an extra credit assignment with each lesson that you hand in.

So, if you work is acceptable and your extra credit is done correctly, Miss Peachtree would consider giving you a passing grade. In the meantime, you are grounded until we say that you are not grounded. Go up to your room until it's time for supper," said his mother.

James was very angry with Ralph. He wondered if he did it on purpose. He decided to confront Ralph the next day.

"Ralph, I failed my test because of you. I would like an explanation."

"I took the test just as you asked me to. Besides, I really was against it from the beginning," protested Ralph. Even Miles was totally shocked. He'd thought that Ralph knew just about everything.

"Let's look at some examples. Take question six for example. The problem was a number line laid out in the form of a ruler. The problem asked for the total distance that a marble travelled between two points on that line. The marble moved from the point eight to the point twelve. The question was, how far did the marble go?" said James.

"Why, the answer is obviously four," said Miles.

Ralph put down three as the answer," replied James.

"Yes, that is right. Three is the answer," said Ralph.

"How do you figure Ralph?" asked James.

"As they asked in the question look at the number line itself. They asked, what was the difference between the number eight and twelve. Right?" asked Ralph.

"Right," they all answered together.

"We look at the numbers themselves. We have the numbers eight, nine, ten, eleven, and the number twelve. The numbers in between are nine, ten and eleven. Those are the numbers between eight and twelve. That is only three," Ralph proclaimed.

"All right, look at number twenty-two," said a frustrated James. "It states that there are two trains that are four hundred miles apart from each other. One train begins its trip at noon and reaches a speed of fifty miles an hour. The other train also begins at noon, but it reaches a speed of one hundred miles an hour. The question asks how long of a time period before the two trains meet each other. You got that wrong too," James said.

"I saw the answer that they wanted me to come up with, but it would have been quite incorrect," said Ralph.

"How would that answer be wrong?" asked James.

"The question didn't take up the possibility that a time zone could be crossed by one or maybe both trains. It also didn't consider the earth's rotation. If the trains were travelling north and south, there wouldn't be a problem. Instead, the trains were to travel east and west. The train travelling east is going against the rotation with the result that it is travelling somewhat slower. But a train going west is going with Earth's rotation and would be somewhat faster and——-"

James rudely cut Ralph off, knowing that he could not argue with the alien on the same level.

"Let's eat so that we can have a little time on the playground," complained James. After some time on the playground, James was in a slightly better mood. He would just have to swallow his pride and actually put some effort into his work.

After their recess, the students found their seats again. Miss Peachtree had yet another announcement for the class.

"It may be that some of your parents have already told you, it seems that our little town will be celebrating a very significant event soon. That event is the one hundred and fiftieth anniversary of the town's founding. To help in that celebration, the town council is holding a contest for our school. The students are invited to submit an essay that could be no longer than one hundred and fifty lines long in which the student would describe why the founding of the city is important to him or her. You have until Friday to turn in your paper. In the meantime, let's work on some social studies," said Miss Peachtree.

After classes let out, they came together to talk before they had to go home for the night.

"Is anybody interested in entering that stupid contest?" asked Miles.

"Not me," said Jenny. "How about you Gary?" He didn't answer because his mind was off somewhere in space.

"James, how about you, are you going to write an essay? You're pretty good at such things as that, "Miles said.

"I've got bigger things to worry about. I've been grounded, and for how long I don't have any idea," griped James.

"That means that the rest of us won't see you this weekend, doesn't it?" asked Jenny.

"We were going to Ralph's place to see if we can help him in anyway. That's too bad. Guess we'll see you Monday, here comes my ride," said Jenny.

CHAPTER NINETEEN

It was a long weekend for everybody, especially James who was stuck at home, Ralph was no further in his quest to return to his home, and the gang felt totally helpless to help them. There was one bright spot, however, for one of the gang's own members. On Monday morning, after attendance, Miss Peachtree gave the order for the students to listen up.

"It is my great honor and privilege to announce the winner of the essay contest. We should all be proud that the winner is sitting here in this very room," bragged Miss Peachtree.

"Will the following student please stand up? That student will read his essay in front of an audience at the hall. Will Gary please stand up?" said Miss Peachtree. Miles and the rest of the group stared at each other in disbelief.

"Congratulations, Gary. You will be scheduled to read your piece at seven o'clock Friday evening. You might want to arrive a half hour early in order to prepare yourself. Let's all settle down and get back to yesterday's lesson," said the teacher.

Gary was unusually quite throughout the morning, and at lunchtime, he said very little.

"Why are you so quiet, Gary? If that were me, I would rub it in certain people's faces. What's the matter anyway?" asked Miles. At first, Gary wouldn't answer. But after the rest of them pressured him, he finally gave in and answered them.

"I'm afraid of large groups of people. There is no way that I will stand up and read my paper," Gary warned.

"But you have to. That was part of the deal," Jenny said. Gary's mind was totally made up and he didn't want to argue any longer. But suddenly an idea came to him.

"Ralph, could you do me a favor and ___" but Jenny and James rudely interrupted him.

"Don't do it, Gary! Don't even think it!" they cried.

"You don't know what I'm about to ask Ralph for," protested Gary.

"Whatever it is, it's not worth the price," said James. But Gary was determined anyway.

Ralph did not say anything. But he began to sense something was terribly off with Gary.

"Would you take my place for the reading of my essay Ralph?" asked Gary.

"I think not. It's your paper. I do not have the right to take your place. You deserve the sole honor of reading your essay," Ralph said.

"I don't care anything about that, I'm totally frightened of being in front of an audience. It happened when I was in the first grade. I was in a play and I forgot my line and I froze up," explained Gary.

"That's true, someone had to come up on stage and carry Gary offstage. They had to stop the show, it was totally embarrassing," added Jenny. But Gary begged and begged Ralph until he caved in.

"Ralph, all that I'm asking you to do is just read my paper and nothing else. What could possibly go wrong?" asked Gary.

"All right, but that will be all that I will do and nothing more," warned Ralph.

Jenny tactfully changed the subject and she asked Ralph how his repairs were going.

"Not good. I could use some more of what you call solder, but I am not very hopeful," said Ralph sadly.

"Oh, wait a minute, Ralph. I was able to sneak into my dad's lab the other night. I was able to grab a couple of these. My father called them transistors. It's the latest invention. If you can make use of them, go ahead and take them. If he asks me about them, I will figure out something," said Jenny. The alien looked at them very closely, then put them gently in his shirt pocket.

"Hey before we all take off; I want to give my essay to Ralph so he can look at it before the presentation. Just read it as written and it will be fine," said Gary as he handed the essay over to the alien. Ralph and Gary headed for their homes before it became too late to be out. Ralph went his way and Gary went his.

But Gary was barely inside his house when his father angrily confronted him.

"What are you doing in the garage? You know that your mother and I don't want you outside after dark by yourself, it isn't safe."

"I just want some peace and quite when I do my homework. That's how I came upon the winning essay to be read at the town celebration. Look at this letter from my teacher." After reading the letter, his parents were in a much better mood, but they still forbade Gary from going out to the garage by himself after nightfall.

Apparently, Ralph barely escaped being found out when one cold morning, the family car failed to start. Gary's dad went to the garage to get some tools. He noticed a light was left on. He went to investigate, and found some empty food plates and some magazines lying on the floor. It was a very close shave. It was pure luck that Ralph wasn't there.

CHAPTER TWENTY

The night finally came for the reading of Gary's composition. The gang found an opportunity to visit Ralph before he was to leave with Gary's family. Ralph was given a set of clothes to wear for the event. But before he had a chance to change into them, James was badgering him to show them how he changed shaped.

"C'mon, Ralph, show us how you do it!"

"That is the one thing that I will not do. Please do not ask me again," said a very serious alien.

"All right, then if you do not show us, then tell us how you do it," asked James.

"First, you must have the image of the person you wish to imitate firmly set in your mind. Next you must surround your entire body with positive ions and …" Jenny interrupted Ralph rather rudely.

"Your planet must be made out of ions. I have to go now, my parents are waiting for me to come home so we can go as a family," said Jenny. Then the rest of them left.

When they arrived they found the hall totally packed. After all, it was a small town in the middle of the winter. Any excuse to get out and do something was not wasted. Ralph soon arrived and he found his way backstage to prepare himself.

Miles and the rest of the group found their seats in the hall and waited for Ralph's introduction. The crowd was getting rather antsy because they wanted to get back to partying.

It was no less than the mayor himself who came onstage to address the crowd.

"Thank you for coming out to celebrate the founding of our illustrious town. We have here a bright young man who will read the winning paper of why it is so important to him. Please give your full attention to him. I give you Mister Gary Reinholt," said the mayor.

"Oh brother," groaned Jenny. Ralph stepped up to the podium and began speaking.

The whole speech lasted for only about fifteen minutes, but at the end of those fifteen minutes, the audience was on its feet. The friends couldn't believe it.

"Unbelievable! How is it that an alien from outer space has more enthusiasm for our town than the rest of us?" groaned Jenny.

Ralph didn't wait for the applause to die down before he found his way to the refreshment table. James and Jenny were quite jealous, not only because of the attention that was for Gary, but also because Gary didn't seem to be suffering any great consequences like they suffered.

When Gary's family had enough celebrating, they decided that it was time to head on home. Even after they all had climbed into the family car, not one of them were aware that Gary was not among them.

When the car pulled up to the house they began to file into the driveway. Without thinking, Ralph headed for the old garage where the real Gary was hiding out.

"Where are you going, Gary? It's time to get ready for bed. We all had a long day, so get inside now," said Gary's father. Ralph did as he was told and he waited until he had a chance to relieve Gary.

When Ralph felt it was safe to go, he headed for the back door. He had barely closed the door when Gary's father entered the kitchen to get a glass of water.

An owl had spotted Ralph and stated hooting to alert the others. Gary's father came to the window that overlooked the backyard searching for any intruders, but he couldn't see what or who was disturbing them. Ralph, who was clinging to the outside wall, overheard Gary's father talking to himself.

"Maybe it's time to lock up that old garage for good. There's been too many unexplained things happening around here," he said. Ralph grew very concerned. When he finally was able to relieve Gary, Ralph relayed everything he had seen and heard.

"This is serious, Ralph. How far along are your repairs for your ship? If we don't do something soon, we may not be able to protect you much longer," said Gary.

"Agreed. I might be ready to make another try in a couple of nights. Let the others know that we can make another visit to the ship," said Ralph.

"I'll let them know. Monday it is. Get some rest, Ralph, it will all work out someway or another. Get some rest and we'll talk later," Gary said.

The gang met several times that weekend, but it was not just to get together in order to have fun. They were on a mission now. It was not just for Ralph's sake, but theirs also. If it were known that they were hiding a so-called criminal from the start, it would be all over for them. If it were discovered that Ralph was an alien and that they were totally aware of it, what would happen to them then?

Monday came soon enough, and the fourth graders were very unsettled. At their lunch period, Ralph informed the members of their group that he was willing to make another attempt to repair his ship.

"I think that we should meet at the ship's hiding place instead of my place. I don't know how much longer I can hide Ralph," said Gary.

"All right then. We'll meet right after dark and whoever can make it, makes it," said James.

"By the way Gary, did anybody mention anything about the other night?" asked Jenny.

"Uh, uh. Nobody has said a single word to me after the party," said Gary in a rather matter of fact tone. James and Jenny were almost angry with Gary because their schemes blew up in their faces after Ralph took their place. There was no way on planet Earth that Gary was able to escape suffering the consequences of his actions.

Miles decided to bring the conversation back on topic.

"Why don't you show us what you have come up with so far and let us know in what way we can help you, Ralph?"

"I mostly need someone to stand guard while I install my repairs. It's more important now that nobody discovers me or my ship," said Ralph. He walked over to his chair and he pulled out a bright and shining module from behind it.

"It's a beautiful thing, Ralph, but do you think that it will hold up this time?" asked James.

"I will give it a try," Ralph said. They all knew that it would only be a matter of time before Ralph would be discovered. They were becoming desperate. They had to act quickly.

CHAPTER TWENTY-ONE

Gary was almost ready to run off and help Ralph repair his ship when the telephone began ringing.

"Gary, could you answer that?" asked his mother.

"Okay. Did you remember that I have a science project that I need to finish with the others tonight?" asked Gary.

"You sure have a lot of science projects in the fourth grade," said Gary's mother in an annoyed type of way.

"It's for you mom," Gary said and she took the receiver from him. Gary waited around a bit because he thought that he had recognized a teacher's voice from school. The conversation seemed to go on and on and as it did so, Gary became more and more nervous. He simply did not remember doing anything wrong.

Finally, the call ended, and his mother put the receiver back on the phone. But instead of looking angry there was a smile on her face. Gary was not a bit less nervous because he couldn't remember doing anything all that great either.

"That was the seventh grade teacher who called," his mother said.

"What did he want with you?" wondered Gary.

"He wanted my permission," she said.

"Permission for what?" he asked.

"They were so impressed by your reading of your essay that they wanted the go-ahead to enroll you in the new debate club after school," said his mother rather proudly.

"I can't speak before crowds, remember what happened to me in the first grade?" protested Gary.

"He thought that you had gotten over that very nicely. In fact, he said that you had developed a kind of charisma," his mother said very proudly.

"There is no way," protested Gary.

"You will have to come up with a better argument than that if you're to get ahead in this world. You start in two weeks and that's that," said Gary's mother.

"I'm not gonna!" bawled Gary.

"Bup!" cried his mother. The decision was already made and that was that. It was getting dark fast outside, meaning he was late in meeting the gang. Gary was in no mood to fight with his mother over something that had not happened yet. All Gary wanted to do at that moment was to assist Ralph any way that he could.

"I'll be home for dinner later," Gary told his parents. He rushed off, not explaining where he was going. "Later!" He tried his best not to draw any attention to himself or to where he was going.

When he arrived at the dunes Miles and Jenny were already standing guard, looking for nosy intruders. Jenny suggested he should find Ralph and ask him what he wants done.

He found Ralph standing by his ship holding the the remote that operated his ship in his hand. Ralph then pushed whatever button that opened the door of the ship. As before, the snow and sand fell away and the panel slowly but steadily opened up.

A dim glow began to shine, then Ralph disappeared inside. Nothing happened for a minute or so, and that made James and Gary very anxious. Then a faint hum was heard from inside the ship. It grew louder.

"It looks like Ralph really did it this time," said James. A few moments later though, the humming stopped and the interior light went dark.

"Why didn't you take off for your planet, did something go wrong? Didn't your repair work?" asked James.

"My power reserves were depleted. I have to let them build back up. I think that my new repairs could hold but I think that it would be better to go slowly so that I do not burn out the new module," said Ralph. "Let us go home."

"We should go and tell the others and head home. I don't need any more flak from my parents and I'm sure you don't either," said Gary. After a brief explanation, the gang headed for home in deep disappointment. On the way, Ralph decided to break the silence.

"Since once again, I have a little time here, I feel obligated to offer a favor to you, Miles. I have done favors for the rest of you. It is only right that I do the same for you, Miles," said the alien.

James and Gary and Jenny all yelled at once. "Don't do it, Miles!" they cried.

"You don't know what you're getting yourself into!" Jenny said.

"Yes, you will regret it for a long time," said Gary. But Ralph felt that he needed to make the offer for Miles.

"Even though I protested, I did as you asked me to for the rest of you. It simply would not be fair to Miles to ignore him. Unlike you others, I am offering a favor of my own free will. It is only fair. I don't have much time left here. So, Miles, what can I do for you?" Ralph said.

"Well… My cousins are holding a family reunion this Friday. They do not get along with our side all that great. Would you be willing to go in my place?" asked Miles.

"Give me the details and I'll see what I can do," said Ralph.

"You'll regret it, Miles," warned James. But Miles could not be persuaded not to take Ralph up on his offer.

But suddenly—-

Bark! Bark! Bark!

They all instantly recognize the sound of Ole Blue.

"Run for it!" yelled Gary.

"Who's there! Show yourself or it will go very badly for you. Show yourself!" demanded the sheriff. He had heard Ole Blue barking and decided to investigate.

Miles had made it into a nearby forested area while the others who were not so quick hid themselves among the other dunes. The were very lucky that Ole Blue still had his leash around his neck.

The sheriff came to where they had just been and he had to struggle to keep the animal under control. All that there was to see were footprints that went in every direction.

"We're really in for it now," James whispered to Jenny. "Blue used to be our friend. To think how he had turned on us. It was nice knowing you all, my parents are going to lock me up in my room and throw away the key," moaned Gary.

"Get ready, the sheriff is headed this way!" warned James. The closer that Blue got, the more he snarled and yelped.

Then a miracle happened. The sheriff suddenly yanked the dog's leash, preventing him from going forward. Fortunately, the sheriff had enough of what he considered false alarms which he figured this also had to be.

"C'mon. There is nobody out here this late in the day. It's probably some rabbit or possum that you smell, let's go find your owner." He dragged Blue by his restraint growling and foaming at the mouth.

"See ya!" and Jenny disappeared into the inky darkness.

"I guess we better 'see ya' before we get caught," said James as he ran off leaving Gary to fend for himself.

That was not the end of Gary's close calls that day. Later in the evening, he had just finished putting together Ralph's dinner and was headed for Ralph's hiding place when his father saw him and called out to him.

"Gary, where are you going with that?" he yelled. Gary was smart in that he had put Ralph's meal in a large brown paper bag to conceal it.

"Um… I'm taking out the trash," replied Gary.

"Oh okay, I thought you were sneaking out to the garage for a moment," said his father. Gary walked over to the trash can and pretended to place the bag inside it. It would only be a matter of time now before Ralph would be discovered. Ralph would have to wait a little longer for his food. Gary hoped along with the other three friends that the spaceship would recharge soon.

CHAPTER TWENTY-TWO

It was decided that if someone wanted to communicate with Ralph, it would be done through the passing of notes in order to keep personal contact to a minimum. Nonetheless, Ralph was determined to carry out his promise to Miles and go in his place to the family reunion despite dire warnings from the group for Ralph made a promise and he was determined to carry it out.

Came Friday evening and Miles managed to sneak up to Ralph's room.

"If you don't want to go through with this, I would certainly get it," offered Miles apologetically.

"I mean what I said and that's it," replied Ralph. Miles prepped the alien and provided the clothes to wear to the party. Miles saw Ralph off, and he hid in the dark room with only a flashlight so that he would not be discovered. At least Ralph would have something to eat other than sandwiches. Still, it was worth it. After all, if one of them found themselves on an alien planet, they hoped that he or she would be treated as friend and not foe. And maybe if one day an invading army should arrive, they would go by because they would have a good reputation by the way they treat strangers.

Because of what had happened at the lake, they were unable to go near the spaceship because of the increased patrols of not only by the police, but the concerned citizens also. Jenny, because she lived the closest to the lake, visited the sand dunes to see how easy or more correctly, difficult it was to get to the space craft. It didn't look good. It was decided that an emergency meeting was to be held at James' parent's house in their basement.

"What do you think, Ralph, do you feel that your ship will be charged up enough for you to fly off towards home?" asked Jenny.

"I am pretty confident that it would have enough charge to start for home," Ralph said.

"The dunes are being watched. Once we get there, Ralph, you should get inside your ship and take off right away. I don't think that there is any way to do this but to just get in and go!" James said.

Jenny was dying to know what dire consequences that Miles suffered because Ralph took his place at his family's reunion. She felt quite smug and more than a little curious about what would happen to Miles, so she briefly changed the subject.

"Hey Miles, what kind of trouble did you get into over at the reunion?" chuckled Jenny.

"What do you mean?" Miles asked.

"Didn't you get yelled at or have your mother receive a call from your cousins or anything like that? No dates or being grounded, nothing?" chuckled Jenny.

"Nothing. What did you expect?" asked Miles. By that time, all of their faces stopped smiling, surely something had to have gone wrong.

"Are you sure? You're not fibbing to us, are you?" asked James

"Nope," was Miles only reply.

"Well Miles, if nobody could tell you apart from Ralph, then that confirms our suspicions about you," said Jenny.

"And so exactly what would that be?" asked Miles.

"It means that you came from outer space too," Jenny joked. Miles did not laugh, nor did Ralph. In fact, he did not react at all. The subject was quickly dropped. Jenny and the others realized that Miles would probably not suffer the consequences like they did because Miles did not intentionally take advantage of Ralph at least not in the way that the others had. Their faces grew red, maybe they felt some embarrassment for the moment at least.

"All right listen up; a storm is moving in tomorrow. This might be our only chance to make this thing happen. Failure is not an option. Time is running out for Ralph. Gary said that his dad is planning on using the garage soon," said James.

"I can't make it tomorrow, my mom is taking me shopping for new school clothes," whined Jenny.

"You had better find a way to help out, we are all in this together. If one goes down, we all go down," warned James. He stood silently with his arms folded across his chest waiting for an answer from Jenny.

"All right, all right, let's enjoy the rest of our time together. I brought some cake for everybody," said Jenny.

The next day, Ralph was nowhere to be seen. Doubtless he was busy preparing for his long journey home. The gang was hopeful for Ralph, but it was a sad day too. The plan was that they meet Ralph in Gary's backyard and then race off to the waiting spaceship. There was absolutely no time for sentimental goodbyes, and it was Ralph's job to jump into his ship and take off and nothing else.

As the day went on, it became apparent that the weather forecast for snow was accurate. A cold wind began to blow from the north and the sky became cloudier and grayer. This also meant that it would turn dark early.

Approximately an hour before the dark would set in. Ralph took one last visit to his room to remove any traces of his being there and to grab the remote that operated the ship's controls which he put in his coat pocket.

Ralph waited outside of the garage so that they could just run off towards the sand dunes. Gary's father came in and out of the house as though he was looking for something, but Ralph was able to remain out of sight. He wished that his friends would come soon.

As Ralph nervously waited for his friends to arrive, it started to snow. It was just a few stray flakes at first then there was more and more of them. They would be able to work unseen behind the thick white curtain of snow.

Then he heard a loud whisper calling out his name.

"We're all here Ralph, we gotta go now," said James. Once again and hopefully for the very last time, they headed for the lake shore. As they got there, Jenny took charge.

"Ralph, run to your ship and get going as fast as you can, Miles and Gary go with him to make sure that everything goes off as planned," she said. Then they ran out into the storm. It was going according to plan now, so Jenny and James stood as lookouts, finally being able to relax a little bit.

Bark! Bark! Bark! Bark! "This cannot be happening!" yelled Jenny. As it was, Jenny had the ability to think quickly on her feet. James, who considered himself to the supreme leader of the group, started to balk at Jenny's command. But she seemed to have a definite plan, so he wisely let her carry it out. Besides, if it failed, he could always pass the blame.

This time, it was the sheriff himself holding the reins on Blue. It was just bad timing for the gang that he was walking along the lakeshore.

"James, take this bag with you, it has some metal containers and some tools. Should I give you the word, start banging as loud as you can to distract the sheriff. I'm going to hide behind that big tree there and I will try to distract Blue. Go behind that big dune over there and wait for my signal," said Jenny. James raced off while Jenny hid behind the tree.

Blue's barking became menacingly louder. Jenny was very smart in planning for something like Blue showing up. She reached into a small paper bag which contained some scraps left over from dinner. She reached into the bag and pulled out a half-eaten chicken leg.

Jenny flung the treat as far as she could in a direction directly opposite of the ship's location.

"Chew on that, Blue!" The sheriff wasn't much of a match for the animal as he dragged him in the wrong direction towards his tasty reward. In no time at all, Blue found the food and scarfed it down in one swallow. Jenny thought Blue would take much longer than that to find his treat so Jenny started to panic somewhat, but she was not one to give up so easily. She found another tidbit and tossed it in another direction. The same thing happened.

Jenny was running out of food. So now it was time for plan B. She had one scrap of food left. She took it and threw it as far as she could not caring where it landed. Then she fled to James's hiding place behind the sand dune.

"Start banging as loud as possible, James!" Then he made all of the noise that he possibly could. The sheriff turned around and headed for the racket.

"Let's go James and find the rest of them." Then they ran until they found Ralph sitting in his pilot seat, gearing for takeoff.

Before Ralph could take off, Gary handed the alien a plain package. Ralph reached inside to find an unopened bag of sugar. "Something to remember us by," said Gary. Once again, Blue was on the trail.

"Thank you for what you have done for me." Then he closed the panel to his spaceship and it began to hum loudly.

"Head for the trees yelled Gary and they fled to the safety of the forest. The ship slowly levitated off of the ground then whoosh, the spaceship soared off trailing a shower of sparks behind it.

From their hiding place, they saw the sheriff come to the spot where Ralph had just taken off from. He stood there in great amazement.

"I hope that Ralph makes it home all right," said James.

"Yeah, me too. See ya," said Jenny as she ran off for home.

"I guess we had better see ya before we get into any more trouble," said James. Then they all ran off.

The next night they really didn't know how to feel about it all. They were happy but yet sad at the same time.

"I hope Ralph made it home safely," said James.

"Yeah, me too," said Jenny. The atmosphere was made even more sad because the sun had dropped below the horizon. The darkening skies became a dark purple. As they looked on there came what appeared to be some sort of comet. It flew directly over their heads.

"Did you see that?" marvelled Miles.

"I didn't see nothing," said James.

"Neither did I. Time to go home," said Gary. Then they all left for home.

This story is dedicated to the memory of
Joyce Dwornicki
who was a most loving mother, grandmother, and friend.

www.ingramcontent.com/pod-product-compliance
Lightning Source LLC
Chambersburg PA
CBHW052143150726
48002CB00003B/1046